THE BLONDES OF WISCONSIN

THE
BLONDES
OF WISCONSIN
ANTHONY
BUKOSKI

The University of Wisconsin Press

Publication of this book has been made possible, in part, through support from the Brittingham Trust.

The University of Wisconsin Press
728 State Street, Suite 443
Madison, Wisconsin 53706
uwpress.wisc.edu

Gray's Inn House, 127 Clerkenwell Road
London EC1R 5DB, United Kingdom
eurospanbookstore.com

Printed in the United States of America
This book may be available in a digital edition.

Library of Congress Cataloging-in-Publication Data
Names: Bukoski, Anthony, author.
Title: The blondes of Wisconsin / Anthony Bukoski.
Description: Madison, Wisconsin : The University of Wisconsin Press, [2021]
Identifiers: LCCN 2020035033 | ISBN 9780299331146 (paperback)
Subjects: LCSH: Polish Americans—Fiction. | LCGFT: Fiction. | Short stories.
Classification: LCC PS3552.U399 B55 2021 | DDC 813/.54—dc23
LC record available at https://lccn.loc.gov/2020035033

For Kathryn M. Lang, my editor of many years

CONTENTS

THE
BLONDES
OF WISCONSIN

TRIBUTARIES

Who ever notices Mr. Urbaniak? He picks up the mail, buys his coffee at the convenience store, and drives off to deliver bills, letters, magazines, and advertising circulars to country mailboxes. During his journey, the rural-route carrier might think about Forever stamps, about the changing water levels on Lake Superior, maybe, of all things, about a Slovak church from long ago. Disconnected thoughts, but the mind of a man like this wanders everywhere. The story goes that in its sanctuary and vestibule the Slovak church had had two stoves made from oil drums. The priest heated them with coal he'd scavenged from the nearby railroad tracks. Because the tiny church held so few parishioners and stood twenty feet from the tracks, someone had given it the grandiose name "Soo Line Cathedral." Do you see what I mean about disconnected thoughts?

There'd been this church plus five other ethnic parishes in Superior, Wisconsin. Now all but one had been shuttered by order of the bishop. As much as Walter Urbaniak was interested in postage stamps or in rivers (this being about tributaries), he was also interested in ecclesiastical and clerical matters, the heating of the stoves in the Soo Line Cathedral.

Catholics aren't the only worshipers in Superior. Lutherans, Methodists, Presbyterians, and Baptists were troubled when their churches closed.

As for the Jews, a sad fate had befallen them. After standing one hundred years in the north end of town, the Agudas Achim synagogue was gutted by fire, and Temple Beth El eventually closed. With synagogues gone, churches gone, no one could hear Hebrew, Russian, Lithuanian, Polish, or Czech in Superior. No synagogues, no churches, no immigrants. Nothing in this lonely corner of the state.

When the postman bemoaned the condition of the world, his wife encouraged him to attend a service in Duluth. The announcement in the paper called it a Remembrance Service, *Yom HaShoah*. "I looked it up. Temple Israel's on the hillside on East Second Street."

"What's being remembered there?" he asked.

"You tell me. You're the history lover."

"So I am," he said. "There's too much to remember. By the time I get them, the stamps on the letters have been canceled. Add to that the junk mail that says Urgent Reply Requested. Time Sensitive Material. Open Immediately. Everything's dated by the time I deliver it."

"It's more for you to think about," she said.

"Yes, more history," the postman replied.

Now I should note that the country hereabouts, the ninety miles Mr. Urbaniak drove each day, is pretty much forests and fields, swamps and bogs. Water drains slowly through clay. It might take thousands of years for rainwater and snowmelt to percolate into the earth. For some time, he'd been thinking about this percolation problem. He was sure that where the Narew River flows to the Bug River in Poland, where water might seep easily through the soil, his grandparents had depended on merchants like those who'd once owned stores in Superior—Edelstein, Cohen, Lurye, Kaner, Sher, Goldfine, Arnovich.

When he was out on County Road C, he called his wife to ask again about the service. "When does it start? Are you sure I can go?"

"'All are welcome,' it says. It's a newer building, cream-colored brick, white trim. I bet it's got a great view of the lake," she said.

4

After work, he told her, "I'll take my car in case you or the boys need the other one."

"You aren't tired? You've driven all those miles."

"Sure, I'm tired," he said, wondering how to explain things to her when she wasn't interested in the past. As a rural carrier, he heard no one for eight hours unless he remembered aloud the Forever stamps the post office had issued, in which case he was speaking to himself. It would have been good talking to Harriet at the end of the day, but by then the postman and his wife were accustomed to silence. The house was quiet on weekends, too. That's how things had gotten with the Urbaniaks.

The car had a caution light. A sign in the rear window read MAIL DELIVERY. A bumper sticker warned VEHICLE MAKES FREQUENT STOPS.

When he entered the temple, a thirty-minute drive from the East End of Superior, children played in a hallway. After inquiring what he wanted, a secretary said, "The children study Hebrew one day a week in case you're wondering." A girl ran up to them. "Have you seen Isaiah?" she asked.

"Hurry along," the secretary replied. To Mr. Urbaniak, it sounded like "*Gey shpil.*"

A child could understand her, whereas when he tried pronouncing words in another language, he could only recall parts of Polish sayings. One was related to a month that had come and gone. It started, "Gdy mróz w lutym ostro trzyma—If frost holds fast in February, winter will be short." All his life, he'd been forgetting the sayings the more things crowded his mind. Then when another postal rate hike came, the Forever stamp reminded him of what had been lost. No ethnic churches. No *Gorzki Żale* services. No Polish carols at Christmas in Superior. What is a man who doesn't remember his past?

When people entered the sanctuary with its altar and tapestried wall, Mr. Urbaniak imagined them wondering, "Who's this? He must be very cautious. He has a yellow light on his car." The woman he'd met downstairs walked in with the language students. Seeming not to notice him, old men passed by him and a mother and son who'd traveled some distance in order to remember. Businessmen were here and the young woman he took to be the Hebrew-language teacher. Soon, fifty people filled the pews.

"What better way to recall the past than through weekday prayer?" the rabbi asked when he entered. On the website, he wore colorful robes. Now, he had on a gray suit, white shirt, a tie. "'The Prayer of the Heart' substitutes for the temple in Israel when we cannot be there," he said. After he read from the *Daily Prayer Book*, he opened the photocopied program to begin the "Readings for *Yom HaShoah*."

The readers had been assigned. "Each prayer to be read by one of the candle lighters," the rabbi had written. The boy who'd traveled here with his mother began. "We remember our dead, who died when madness ruled the world and evil dwelt on earth." He lit a candle on the table in front of the rememberers, then placed it in a holder. The smell of wax and smoke hung in the air.

The young man sitting ahead of Mr. Urbaniak read a paragraph. Without looking up, he said, "We mourn for all that died with them, their goodness and their wisdom."

A middle-aged woman read. Fumbling with her glasses, an older woman with a cane said, "We salute those who were not Jews, who had the courage to suffer with us. They are your witnesses." After the two lit candles, another candle lighter walked up, then another.

After the "Mourners Kaddish for *Yom HaShoah*," which sounded ancient and haunting to Mr. Urbaniak, the rabbi said, "Turn to the last page of your programs."

The list of names in the postman's program read: "DeJongh, Rachel—From the Netherlands. Engel, Hugone—From Hungary." When the place of residence wasn't known, the program said: "Perished at Bergen-Belsen. Perished at Neuengamme."

Fifty-four names. He listened to others in the temple read them: "Kalman, Jolan—From Slovakia. Sieke, Walter—From Germany. Schaechter, Flora—From Romania." An evening of candles, the sound of names. "Klein, Ilona. Shichtman, Martin. Pomush, Lev." He wished they'd come to America and lived on the rural route. How he wished and wished that things were different.

But here he was daydreaming. He thought about the time by the cemetery near the Point of Rocks where he'd seen an old man from church weeping as he tended a grave. Now Mr. Urbaniak thought of other names. The eighty-three thousand murdered at Auschwitz, Catholics whose identity was never mentioned in the news or in the history books. They were among the "others" killed in the Nazi camps along with Gypsies, intellectuals, homosexuals. No one ever said their names.

"Wait!" he said. Accustomed to sorting and delivering mail, he surprised himself. As the word echoed, people looked up. "I'm Walter Urbaniak. St. Adalbert was the patron saint of my church before it closed. He's the patron saint of Poland. My father came from the old country. He told me about things."

"Patron saint?" the rabbi asked.

"I want you to know this so I can add my names," said Mr. Urbaniak. "Where are the Catholics no one knows about? Listen to *my* names." He thought he should stop; but, tired of being cautious, he couldn't stop, not this time. As for the congregation, it was as if they wanted to hold onto the moment when an outsider interfered with their lives. "Wait?" the temple-goers muttered. They shook their heads. Someone insulted him. The rabbi looked puzzled.

This might seem odd to tell at a moment when a Catholic postman interrupted a service in a temple, but some years earlier his neighbor had sent money to the old country for a type of water advertised as health restoring. If you know about the garden next door to the Urbaniaks' house and the phonograph music the boy, Alphonse Bronkowski, played there, then you'll know the story of the water from thousand-year-old springs. The Bronkowskis had had what you would call a memory garden. On summer nights, a passerby or a neighbor would hear Chopin or Paderewski playing from a phonograph among the flowers. Sometimes, he would hear Count Michał Ogiński's stirring "Farewell to My Country . . . *Pożegnanie Ojczyzny*."

When he was ill late in life, the postman's father, Adam Urbaniak, had thought that listening to the music and drinking the water would cure him. *Nałęczowianka Naturalna Woda.* On the green-and-white label, a manor house nestled in the kind of forest you'd find on a rural postal route. How can spring water flow for centuries without stopping? As the water in the bogs and swamps of northern Wisconsin seeped into the earth, the water in the old country rose to the surface. As the Polish names went through his head, he thought of those who had died, been sent to gulags, or been exiled after the war like his neighbors, Mr. Bronkowski, Mr. Bronisław Slinker, the Pogozalski sisters.

"Wait?" the rabbi said. He looked like he could be very powerful when angry. "Wait?" he repeated, using a Polish word—"*Czekać*"— Mr. Urbaniak had forgotten. The way the rabbi came toward him frightened the postman.

The next day, alarmed by what had happened, Mr. Urbaniak, a harmless one for all that, said to his wife, "Tell the boys to bring me the water."

"The water didn't help your father's health," his wife reminded him.

"Tell the boys something needs to be done," he said.

"What are you up to? Those places you go on your mail route. You're alone too much. What have you dreamt up this time?"

"I'd wanted to say something yesterday. I was wondering why *our* people aren't remembered. When I said 'Wait,' everyone stared. There was no point going on with the request, so I followed the rabbi when he motioned to me. I thought he'd walk me to the car, maybe even call the police, but he had me do something else."

"You poor, poor Walter! That's all you got from this service?" his wife asked.

"No, you don't understand."

As Mr. Urbaniak wrapped the bottles of water in paper to keep them from breaking, he said, "He had me read."

Remembering his father saying "A dry April doesn't give much hope," he brought the program from the temple with him when he left.

The gravel road goes through a valley by the Pokegama River then up into a forest. The gravestones at the top of the hill stand close together as if to protect them from the outside world. The postman was mindful of how people destroy things belonging to the living and the dead. Maybe that explains the sturdy fence, to keep people from damaging the Hebrew cemetery. Alone on the hill, he studied the names on the stones, many of them familiar, then he looked at the Hebrew writing.

Below some distance, the Pokegama River wound through the valley. Despite the cool spring, the aspen trees were budding. Even with the wind picking up, the cemetery was peaceful. No old country saying about April's hopelessness could hold back the new season. On the gravestones, the inscriptions read, "Beloved Father Louis Weinstein," "The Spirit Shall Return Unto God Who Giveth It," and so on. A menorah was carved over the name on the grave of Sarah Benesovitz. Mr. Urbaniak read other names, "Aronsohn, Ansell, Siegel." He wondered whether his ancestors had visited cemeteries in the boggy region of the Narew River in Poland.

Despite his good intentions, he had no business here. Though at the rabbi's bidding people had been polite, Mr. Urbaniak knew how they'd felt. The young girl looking for Isaiah wouldn't have wanted him in the Hebrew cemetery. The old people wouldn't. Realizing he'd been irrelevant yesterday, Mr. Urbaniak imagined how another visitor might have broken the imported bottles so that the sexton, the cemetery caretaker, would find the glass shards and paper labels that read "Nałęcz, Poland."

If he walked down the hill, he'd be off cemetery property. Then he wondered whether boundaries were important when for centuries in Poland Catholic families had been tied to the Jews.

Judging from where he stood on the riverbank and the river's slow current, the Nałęczowianka water would take a half-hour to pass the cemetery. He wondered whether the Narew River ran through clay country like the Pokegama River on the outskirts of town. He twisted field grass into a cone, set it afire, threw the burning grass into the river. As you waited for something more to occur, could you purify yourself of what had happened in another country?

When he'd emptied the bottles of Nałęczowianka water, he read the passage the rabbi had given him yesterday. To allow Mr. Urbaniak to include himself, as though they'd once been neighbors in an old country, Rabbi Epstein had encouraged him to emphasize the word "we" when he'd spoken in the temple. Now he read the part again by the river. "They are like candles which shine out from the darkness of those years, and in their light, we know what goodness is."

Then he read the names, the Polish Jews first. "Khaszewski, Sarah. Bugajski, Solek," he said. Then more names: "Mindel, Lazar—Perished at Natzweiler. Glikman, Jakob—Perished at Buchenwald. Loewy, James—Perished at Dachau."

It would take him forever to think about the people they represented. By then, the water would have flowed on and the other handfuls of burning grass long been extinguished. Even so, he imagined those who'd have passed his Polish ancestors, waving to them on the way to the river, which Mr. Urbaniak now saw was a tributary of a river in Superior, Wisconsin. He remembered very few Polish words, but he knew that nearby in the cemetery was a language that was millennia old. In the language would be the word "we" the rabbi had urged him to use. And in the language might be a word for the man of Polish descent, the Catholic man, who merely wanted to understand how it had once been in an old country.

ENGLISH THROUGH PICTURES

The Sunday newspaper runs a "human interest" story about my dad. It tells how an honest-to-goodness cavalryman from World War Two vacuums dust in a flour mill in Superior, Wisconsin. Over the newspaper caption "Cavalryman rides again" is a photo of Frank Bronkowski getting on the man-lift. The belt with wooden hand- and footholds runs to the sixth floor of the mill and back down. Under a second photo, in the caption below it, my dad says, "The pay isn't much, but the job has good benefits." Dusting off his work shirt in the photo, he cocks the white grain-miller's cap to the side. The article concludes: "When the durum wheat and semolina dust coat everything, Mr. Bronkowski springs into action."

Because of the dust in the mill, my dad is short of breath. After he photographs me at parade rest in our yard this autumn morning, he says, "Stand at attention. Look at the camera and salute." Coughing to clear his lungs, he steadies himself and clicks the Brownie Instamatic so that my folks can remember me in uniform.

"You'll throw out your back. I'll get your corset," Ma says.

As they discuss back support, I prepare for another photo. I wonder whether Mr. Urbaniak, our neighbor, or Mr. Bronisław Slinker, the writer, our other neighbor, is watching. Home on leave after

Marine Corps boot camp, I'm in a service cover with a black visor, a tan shirt and tie, web belt, tan trousers, shined black shoes.

My dad wants me to visit King Midas Flour. With the grinding, milling, and packing floors running nonstop, it's noisy and dusty there. He also wants me to wear my uniform whenever we go out in my uncle's truck with the spray bar on it, my dad's second job.

The next photo is of me, Private Bronkowski, holding my baby brother Ed. "You going to enlist someday?" I ask Eddie as the old man takes our picture. Then Ma takes a picture of me and the old man. During the ordeal of standing here posing, I think of how Willa, my girlfriend, had mailed me pogey bait in boot camp, which can be chewing gum, candy, crackers, anything a recruit isn't allowed to receive. In serious trouble with the drill instructors, I got with the program from then on. After I graduated, completed a month of Infantry Training Regiment, and then flew home, she was supposed to pick me up at the Minneapolis airport in her sister's car.

If trouble comes in threes, I was at two with her. When she didn't show up, I called her once I got home via Greyhound bus. Someone was singing in the background, as if Willa and a mystery man were performing a duet.

"Sounds like someone's there," I said.

"Shh—" she said, putting her hand over the receiver to quiet him.

After that, Willa and I hardly talked. When we watched the high school football team play one night, we stood in the shadows outside the stadium. "I'm going to Okinawa. I'll be away thirteen months. Can I hold your hand at least?" I asked. Her fingers tightened on the chain-link fence. "If you need to talk to someone, call the request line at WEBC," she said. "Ask them to play 'Sukiyaki.'"

In the song, a hit the year before, Kyu Sakamoto, a Japanese man, whistles and looks skyward so his tears won't fall to earth. That's when I realized she was considering areas of human interest that didn't include Private Al Bronkowski, the guy she was going with, the guy she didn't want to be seen with anymore.

...

Today, my dad will apply calcium chloride to roads in the county. The solution settles the dust. When the phone rings and I hope it's Willa, it's my Uncle Pete wanting to know if my dad can work for him today and when do I leave home. "Are you excited about the Marine Corps?" "Affirmative." We'd been cleaning our rifles when a drill instructor told us what'd happened in the Gulf of Tonkin. Boot camp got harder, like we had a game coming up against Hanoi. That's when Private Huber of our platoon went crazy. He was discharged for eating flies. The Lord of the Flies is home now, and maybe after Okinawa I'll be going to Vietnam. Over the phone, Uncle Pete asks again about my dad. "Dust?" I ask. "Yes," Pete says. The side of his truck says, CURE YOUR DUST PROBLEMS. CALL THE GOOD DOCTOR. All week, Uncle Pete has dust on his mind. When Pete can't drive, it's my dad's job.

At 0930 hours, the photo shoot done, my dad and I page through a book Ma'd been looking for in the basement. The book brings up languages from Urdu to Telugu to Vietnamese. Now all I hear about is Vietnam, the Gulf of Tonkin, Ho Chi Minh.

The prefaces read, "This book will teach you the first steps of English. It gives you about 500 important words in sentences, with the meaning shown through pictures." The prefaces say the same thing in different languages. In Dutch, the words "This book will teach you the first steps of English" is "Dit boek zal uw eerste schreden in de Engelse taal leiden," in Finnish, "Tämä kirja opettaa Teille englanninkielen alkuaskeleet." A box with squares inside appears with each preface. Next to the boxes are directions in Hindi, Swedish, Rumanian, Serbo-Croatian, Tagalog. In Portuguese, the sentence "Read each page like this" is "Cada pagina deve ser lida na seguinte ordem."

My dad gets a sheet of paper, a pencil, a ruler. He wants the squares he's about to draw on the paper to look like those in the book. He numbers the four squares as I try to read the Polish preface. "Książka ta nauczy cię początków angielskiego . . ." In *English through Pictures*, each square has a simple picture in it drawn by an artist. My dad will add *his* art, then we'll get the truck from Doctor Dust.

Eleven miles outside of town, Frank Bronkowski opens the $CaCl_2$ jets. The solution comes by barge to Superior from Ludington, Michigan, and Goderich, Ontario. We're spraying Barnes Road when I find drawings like his on the pages of the book. Other pages have drawings of a hat on a bed, a truck on a road. In one picture, there's a clock and beside it the words, "What is the time?" Another picture, one of a cow in a pasture, asks, "What animal is this?" Whether in Bengali, Indonesian, or Thai, the forty-one prefaces promise the English learner, "The sentences will take on meaning as you compare them with the help of the accompanying pictures. The load on your memory is kept light. Your attention can be given to seeing how changes in the sentences go along with changes in the meaning. Learning English this way is more like play than hard work."

When he came to America, my dad had drawn the horse he's sketched again in the kitchen. "Look on the other pages in the book," he says. On four of them are the horse drawings, drawings from another time, plus the book's drawings. He's always drawn the horse the same way.

When he was sent to Krojanty in 1939 to protect the railroad junction, he'd ridden Lotna, he tells me. Even when he's concentrating on calcium chloride, I'll be able to learn about my father. Right now with him preoccupied, I think of the jokes people must've told when they read the newspaper article about him: "How did the Germans conquer Poland? They marched in backward and the Polish thought they were leaving." "What would you call the paper grocery bag Frank Bronkowski brought with him to America? Polish luggage." "How do you stop a Polish cavalry charge? Turn off the carousel." Who doesn't like a joke?

"You see t'ese fields?" he asks as he points to the clover that's been harvested by the man up the road. "In a forest like at the edge of this

14

field, we wait until our commander yelled '*Atak*.' Out of the forest, we rode in the charge at Krojanty, 250 men. The 1st and 2nd Squadrons, we charged across the plain in the dust. We lost the colonel and twenty men, but nobody care."

"The newspaper cared. It wrote about you. What will go in the empty squares following the horse pictures?" I ask.

Because his English isn't good, it's difficult for him to tell me much. After all these years, he's learning a language he doesn't have time for. His nights working at the mill are hard enough and keeping ahead of the bills and taking care of the house, which my ma can't do much of because of her asthma.

On a morning which my dad says is as beautiful as the one twenty-five years ago in the old country, it's just me and him. Maybe he's riding the carousel in the Polish joke, never telling anyone about the things he did. My dad's face has gotten old in the four months since I've been away. The regiment of lancers is like something from two hundred years ago.

The hissing of the spray bar, the truck's tires on the gravel, my dad's hands on the wheel.

"What's in the squares?" I ask. "You never talk. Please, tell me what you can about the squares." But it's no use. In my imagination, I fill them in. He is a youth. Sword drawn, he's charging the tanks of the armored division. The officers are yelling. The horses are galloping into the noise and dust. Everyone in the cavalry brigade is brave.

"Where you go?" he asks, as if—waking from a dream—he's forgotten I'll be overseas. Now that I know at least a little about the cavalry brigade, about the artist of horses, I'll come to see him in the boiler room at the flour mill. I'll stand at attention to salute the Polish *korporal*.

"All my life, I fill in the squares," he says. "In the first square, I am praying. In second square is enemy. In square three is our charge. In square four—" My dad studies the dashboard gauges as calcium chloride dampens the road.

"What's in square four?" I ask, knowing I'll be thinking of Willa Beecher when the fourth square of my own life comes around. After

Staging Battalion, I'll be on a troop transport. At some time during the year, I'll go to Vietnam. We'll all go, I think.

Sixteen hundred gallons of calcium chloride will dampen a mile of dirt road eighteen feet across. When we're done, I tell my dad that if I go to Vietnam, I'll hide *English through Pictures* along a road. Perhaps a peasant will find it and write his own long history. My father and I are writing our history today as I fill in what I can of his life. When he came here, our priest gave him the copy of *English through Pictures*. For meals, my dad had to sit on the stairs of the first-floor landing of our Polish grade school to wait for what the nuns had prepared for him in the second-floor kitchen.

"Will you drive me to town?" I ask, knowing that at the storage tanks he'll open the vents on the truck to keep the pressure inside from building. He'll attach the hose, punch in the quantity of $CaCl_2$ he'll need for the next run. I can phone Willa. She'll meet me.

I've thought about this for weeks, how she'll ask, "Why'd you go in the service when you didn't have to?"

I wish I was in dress blues when I tell her I'd wanted to escape the dust in Superior. In this daydream I'm having, I'm asking her, "Whose car do I see at your house?" *Jesus, I stood in front of the platoon, gagging on the gum wrapper the DIs made me chew, Willa'd sent the gum, the pogey bait.*

When I realize I'm safe with my father on a dirt road, I think that if I wrote a heading for one part of this October afternoon, it would say, "I'll Go to War." If I wrote a heading for his life, it would say, "What He Amounted To." It would include being president of the Tadeusz Kościuszko Club, the Polish Club, of Superior, Wisconsin, and his friends in the Holy Name Society and the car in the garage and the house.

"What happened when you were young?" I ask him.

At forty-four, the laborer at the flour mill on the bay tells me that in the old country he'd loved the daughter of a millhand. "Neither of us knew anyt'ing about life. We were like you," he says. "Every day, we walked through the fields. Toward the end of summer, we sang 'Farewell to My Country.' We picked wild roses."

As long as his words connect him to the past, we can stay on this road thinking of what goes in the squares. About my dad and the mill-hand's daughter, I imagine that after the war there was no one for him to return to, or if she was waiting in the village near Łomza, her heart had changed. War changes everyone.

Before the attack in 1939, twenty-five years ago, though, two lovers had danced in a field, my dad and the girl from the village. This *did* happen. For a moment, he looks into the future, his heart beating as they walk through the sun-drenched fields.

"Where you go?" he asks me, the awakening soldier.

In the coming months, I'll be in Staging Battalion in California, on Okinawa, then who knows where? When New Year's Day 1965 arrives, I'll write Willa's name in the first square. In a letter, I'll ask her to wait for me. I'll be a good man when I return to the States, I'll write her. When my dad's birthday comes five months after that, May 1965, then Father's Day a month later, I'll calculate the time zones between Superior and the South Vietnam jungle and fill in those squares. I'll be careful on Father's Day to get the precious hours right. I'll fill in squares and be grateful for what he's confided in me.

"The night before I left," my dad tells me, "my mother said she would be very sad without me. 'You will be okay,' I comfort her. Then we don't talk about my going away, as if tomorrow will be like every day. I should have bowed to everyone on our farm. I should have asked their blessing. The next morning, I kiss Grażyna goodbye.

"One of the soldiers called me *Róża Polna* . . . Wild Rose. When I fought him, he stopped laughing at the rose pinned to my shirt. I rode Lotna from then on and thought of the fields of home and my mother, father, and Grażyna. As Poland prepared for war, our country was behind in everything, no planes, tanks, ammunition."

"Would this be in square four?" I ask him.

"The trains came from Chojnice," he goes on, as if in a trance. "Soldiers got off, boys from country villages who were awaiting assignment. But I had my horse and the rose. They were enough.

Then at Krojanty off of the train came an officer with another rose for me from Grażyna."

When I see his face, my father's face older than I've seen it but happy, I realize how much I don't know about Korporał Bronkowski, Łomza, Poland. "How do you say Father's Day?" I ask. "Before I go away, I want to remember you saying it. I know Father's Day is special in Poland. Tell me how you say it. I want the memory of you and me on this afternoon." I turn my head upward so my tears won't fall. I don't know how I can leave him, this beloved man I know little about.

Maybe his tears are falling for me and for himself, for everything he's missed out on. Or perhaps I imagine this and I don't see tears. Maybe he's accepted that I must leave. He's a strong man, my dreaming father, the cavalry soldier. The carousel can play the music of a carnival. As the painted horses rise and fall and rise and fall to a polonaise by Paderewski, Ogiński, Chopin, he'll be on the most beautiful horse of all, the white Arabian, its mane flowing. No one must stop the carousel with him on it, no one must stop the charge into history of the *Pomorska Brygada Kawalerii*, not at this moment when my father is happy to think of the past. He's far ahead of the others in the charge. The earth erupts. For one second, the korporał sees the rose.

Before he answers me twenty-five years later, he clears his throat. "Father's Day? . . . *Dzień Ojca*," he says as the dust settles from the calcium chloride.

THE EVE OF THE FIRST

Written in Polish by Bronisław Slinker, émigré author and resident of Superior, Wisconsin. Translated by Tomasz Malinowski.

Janusz Brozek sold everything in his shop: pins, needles, twine, ribbons. Woolen jackets hung from the walls. Shoes and boots crowded the shelves. Everything was here, household goods, hardware items, fishing and hunting supplies, dresses, lotions, ointments, balms.

Each morning, he'd turn up the lamps, unlock the door, and hang out the sign which read *AUSVERKAUF . . .* SALE. For a while longer, this region on the border was to remain Polish, though more often now Mr. Brozek heard customers saying, "Das Wetter ist sehr kühl und feucht, Herr Brozek" or "Guten Abend, Herr Brozek."

These days when someone said goodbye in German after shopping, he suspected another meaning in their words. Nevertheless, after dusting the countertops and straightening his goods, he enjoyed watching the townspeople hurrying by. There went the children with their schoolbooks, the nuns following them. Housewives walked arm-in-arm. The Jew from three doors away bowed to them. Older boys teased and pushed one another. Seeing Brozek half-hidden in his shop, one of them shaded his eyes to peer in, leaving smudges on the window. The trolley clanged and rumbled past.

No matter the time of day or year, it was shadowy where the gloomy hours tick-tocked by on the old German clock. When a customer entered, the lamps flickered. Otherwise in the stillness, Brozek, a smart businessman, moved this, arranged that, to make his wares more appealing.

In the rear of the shop, his mother sat in a wheelchair with a high cane back. She could name the rivers of northeastern Poland where they'd lived long ago. She'd talk about them all day, the Narew, the Bug, the Biebrza. In one of them, his father had perished, his body never recovered. Now Brozek and Mother were themselves submerged, you might say, in a country whose borders like vast, barren sea straits had changed again since independent Poland had reclaimed her territory from Germany to the west. At least in this place, they were far from the Russians.

Mother would sit in the wheelchair remembering the country to the northeast. Not much passed between mother and son anymore. With talk of a new war frightening *Pan*, or Mister, Brozek, he fixed her shawl or rearranged her lap quilt, asking, "How are you, Mother?" Hearing her whisper something, he'd return to the front of the shop. In his own country, he felt like a foreigner. Life wore heavy on him. Mother stayed in the back not noticing, but Brozek noticed what was happening along the borderland.

The floor-length mirrors he owned seemed lavish for a small shopkeeper. The wooden frames were engraved with flowers, with birds in flight. His dear mother and the mirrors were constants in Brozek's life. Looking in them, he'd think of Poland. He'd wonder about living someday in a city, Warsaw maybe after Mother had died and after he'd sold the shop—God forbid!

When he stood facing a mirror and looked a little to the right or left, he'd see a reflection of himself in the mirror behind him. In the mirror behind, a reflection in front. Here he was, there he was, back and forth reflections, so that the middle-aged Brozek, by placing the mirrors just so, could multiply into ten or more of himself. With Brozek everywhere, he wondered how to become the man at the far end of the reflections, the man of energy and purpose he'd been when business was better. In order for customers to see themselves in a new coat or muffler, he'd direct them before the mirrors. Now he'd found another use for the mirrors. They were more than a way to examine himself in his tweed jacket, celluloid collar, and cravat before opening the door for business. Before proceeding, I should say that Janusz Brozek had such a look of regret. You could see it in the deep-set eyes, the pale lips, the chin less resolute than it had been a few years before. It was a defeated face. A few customers worried that he'd weep as he sold them a hard candy or a paper kite. "Trauriger Herr Brozek... sad Mr. Brozek," they'd said when leaving the shop. On and off for centuries, his country had been at war. Such a troubled history has shaped many sad faces. Brozek, though, had another reason to be sad: He was a romantic without romance. He didn't understand women.

After hours, he turned away from the window, retreating into the back of the store. Hearing him, his mother, who also struggled with life, whispered, "I need more air."

Among those passing outside was Fräulein Helsel, Gisella. For nearly a year, Brozek had seen her about. During this time, he'd also come to realize why *he'd* finally turned inward. At forty-seven, the hope of love, happiness, and marriage were fading. But how could Fräulein Helsel have lost hope? Life was just beginning for her, Brozek thought. Sometimes she'd turn in midstride, returning to his shop or to the shop with the Jewish proprietor three doors away. As she stared at the displays in Brozek's window, he saw the dark lines beneath her eyes, her lips pursed thoughtfully. She'd drum her fingers on the glass.

She wanted a metal cigarette case, a tin matchbox, something a gentleman might enjoy. But when he showed her his stock of things, she wasn't satisfied.

...

21

"I've been under a strain," she said to Brozek one day. That a young woman would confess something to him brightened his spirits. "I fear I'm losing a friend. I don't know what to buy him. Nothing in your shop seems right."

"The thought of war upsets him?"

"He's more excited than nervous."

"Here," said Brozek, "this will calm you." He offered her chocolates. There were dancing German maidens on the tin box.

"I see him changing every day," she said. "He's changed so much. Germany has changed."

Brozek offered her tea. He made a Polish toast as he lifted his cup. "Mother and I came here to escape the Russians. But sometimes it's hard to breathe now. We're used to war. But you're so young," he said.

Lost in dreams, Fräulein Helsel looked over his merchandise. When the clock struck six, she said, "And still I've found nothing. Nothing interests me."

"Don't leave," he said. Beneath a counter, he rummaged for a mirror. "He can admire his armband in this pocket mirror."

"His vanity is his armband and the brown shirt he wears to rallies. My friend says not to come to these shops. If he knew I bought this from you, he'd be angry."

"They've been bothering Mr. Engelmann three doors down. You're German?" asked Brozek.

"Part German, part Polish. I mean harm to no one."

"Nor do I. Can you have a drink with me? It'll be cold when you go."

She was unsure what to do, but Brozek's shop was quiet, the shopkeeper's voice restful after the noisy world she'd grown accustomed to.

That evening when she left with the pocket mirror and he locked up, then prepared a late supper for *Matka* in back; that winter evening, Brozek returned to the shop and smiled into the floor-length mirrors the way he planned to smile for Fräulein Helsel in the future.

"Goodnight, Brozek," he said.

"Goodnight, Brozek," said the shopkeepers who were dressed like him in the mirror. "Goodnight. Goodnight," they replied in unison.

...

What an army of illusion Poland would have if it could muster a thousand such mirrors. One thousand perfectly placed mirrors to look back and forth in. One soldier per mirror. One thousand reflections per soldier: what an army to confound an enemy. When spring came, he'd practice his reflections in ponds and rivers. For the time being, he thought of Gisella Helsel.

Though afraid of being seen, she visited the shop again. His courtesy, his seriousness, the formality with which he spoke, even his stylish jackets made her like him.

"How did he receive the gift?" he asked.

"For a moment, he couldn't bear to see in the little mirror what he's become. He hasn't much time for me. But you, you've no wife?"

"I have Mother. We have the shop. Brozek has Brozek."

"Are you good company for yourself?" she joked.

"My mirrors think so," he replied. "Though I also have great responsibilities, such as Mother's health and the items spread out here." He invited her to see more of the goods. He opened another tin of chocolates with the dancing maidens. He brought out vodka. From a display case, she took a scarf. "Do you really have more mirrors? I'd like to see myself."

"Yes, several," he said.

The mirrors were taller than Fräulein Helsel. He aligned her before them.

Except for the ticking of the old German clock, a portent of war, the shop was still. Looking at her, he said, "Your reflection is lovely." Her hair in a bun, he imagined it undone and falling over the pale blue scarf. His glance fell to her neck, her blouse. He smoothed the scarf. When she turned to see him, he said, "I've been looking here for months. Sometimes I wish I could turn away. But I'm drawn to myself."

He surprised her when he edged so close to the mirror his lips practically touched the glass. Then they did, the two Brozeks merging into one. "Who are you looking for, Janusz?" she asked.

23

"Myself. Can't you see?" he said. "There are armies waiting to charge out of the depths."

"They aren't real."

Brozek didn't know whether to turn back to her or to remain looking in the mirror. "When I admire myself, I whisper, 'Which Brozek are you?'"

"The one before you," said Fräulein Helsel. Noticing the time, she turned to leave. "I can't join you tonight," she said. "I have to meet him."

It was so quiet with her gone that when Brozek said "Poland" the reflections whispered it to him. If you listened, Mother, in her room for the night, could be heard saying, "*Polska, Polska.*"

Insofar as Fräulein Helsel was concerned, what had happened in the shop would never have occurred with her friend, let me call him Klaus, who was in fact her fiancé and not at all interesting to her. If the slump of Brozek's shoulders reflected a defeated man, what of it? Any thoughtful person who saw how things were turning out in Czechoslovakia, Poland, all over Europe, would have to be this way. Klaus wasn't thoughtful. He drank too much.

The shop was a quiet place. Lamps flickered, clothes hung neatly, an old woman sighed to her sons in the mirrors. As I say, depending on how things were aligned, how reflections were aligned, there could be ten, maybe twenty Brozeks working evenings. You'd walk into his shop. He'd invite you to the mirror of your choice. Far away from the drum beaters and hollerers, he'd invite you to kiss yourself.

Presented with a romantic opportunity, Fräulein Gisella Helsel returned. It was the possibility for adventure that brought her to the *Beckenstrasse.* The troubled noises in the streets giving her headaches, she'd stop at the druggist's for powders, then pass the shop three doors down before she came to Brozek's.

"Your coat, let me take it," he'd say. "Here, warm up. How do you do?"

They'd share coffee, chocolates, cigarettes, such preliminaries drawing out the evening.

"*Dziewica* . . . Maiden," Brozek called her. Sometimes to himself,

24

he whispered the name, "*Lalka . . . Doll.*" He considered marriage. But how to know whether she felt as he did?

"What do you want?" his mother would say night after night from the back. "What, Januszka?"

"Only to know if she loves me."

"Wait. It's only March," his mother said. "You know what occurs on St. John's Eve. Animals talk, earth shows her riches. The future is forecast by the flowers and grasses a maiden is to weave. St. John's Eve holds the promise of youth, love, and fertility for you. Wait until then, until St. John's Eve. Wait three months."

"But, Mother, is it going to be all right for me?"

"Yes, Janusz."

Not often did Brozek leave his shop. What was out there but the noise, dirt, and hollering of young Germans? Still, he had a place he returned to a few times a year. He'd come here before with a Polish woman. Was it twenty years ago? They said they loved each other, but it wasn't true. *Trauriger Herr Brozek*, sad Mr. Brozek, had found out about love from her, the bliss that ends quickly. When he came back here, he liked to think of her. It'd been no one's fault what had happened. Or perhaps it was partly his fault. His shop, his business, too many things had gotten in the way of love.

Now when Mother told him about the St. John's Eve rituals, many weeks remained before the linden trees bloomed. He rode the streetcar that swayed and bumped along the rails. Things had changed since he'd journeyed here years before to see a woman in love with him. Today, young men ran in the streets, upset ashcans, painted swastikas on buildings. Neighborhood thugs harangued the Jews when they passed. Workers crowded on and off the streetcar. They shouldered him out of the way. As the car rocked down the streets, its rails squealing, engines rumbled over the land. Biplanes crossed above.

The Gasthaus, which had been here a hundred years, stood on a corner. Inside, his favorite table in the alcove was unoccupied. His elbows resting on the wooden table, he could think of the mistakes of the past and calculate matters regarding Gisella and the future. When he ordered a second and third stein of beer, he saw himself in a mirror that hadn't been here before. He prepared to toast his marriage to the beautiful Fräulein Helsel. He thought of the years they'd be together.

When the weather warmed, she returned to him. Now more comfortable in the shop, she said to the mirror, "*Wo ist das Herz?* . . . Where is the heart?"

"*Serce* . . . the heart," he replied in Polish, pointing to it.

"Point to my heart now," she said.

"*Das Herz,*" he said.

Closer to the day Mother had spoken of, Pan Brozek did another brave thing, especially considering the difficulties of the times: He left the shop again. In doing so, he traded the mirrors and the front window for other depths.

For as long as he'd lived here, he'd come occasionally to a pond surrounded by forests. Springs produced nearly imperceptible ripples on the bottom of the pond, above the springs, the white sand, then the surface. By mid-May of the war year, greenery overgrew the sandy shore surrounding the gentle water. When he swam twenty strokes out, he took a deep breath. Thrusting his face in, he stared below, hoping to see somewhere a shopkeeper's face.

"Janusz, she must make a wreath of flowers and grasses," Mother had said. "On St. John's Eve, she puts the wreath in a pond or river. It will drift toward the man she's to marry."

But St. John's Eve had passed before Brozek in his romantic way mentioned a wreath to Gisella. "Will you do this for me?" he asked one night in the dressing mirrors in back of the shop where even in summer gas lamps flickered. "You weave the wreath of rue, sage, and mullein. You wind and bend the phlox, the white ivy, the St. John's herb to fit the wreath. On it, you place a candle. I have one for you."

He lit it. The light reflected from the front to the back mirrors until he realized that the depths of the mirrors might actually be seen not in inches or feet, but in miles. An Army of Illusion could travel for miles in mirrors.

"You say the smoke of the St. John's festival with its bonfires will keep the witches and hail away from the crops?" she said into a mirror.

"Yes. This is the custom, Gisella," he said. On her forehead, the slight scar from where, as a child, she'd fallen or perhaps cut herself in play. Even this imperfection endeared her to him.

"Then," she said in Polish so that he kissed her hair, "what is expected of me?"

"Do this," he said. "Make this wreath."

The mirrors recorded the summer. Fräulein Helsel finished the wreath—not, however, before the first of July or even August. It was long after the real St. John's Eve on the twenty-third of June that she'd fastened the candle to the wreath. All of July she'd been collecting sundew and mullein, all of August collecting ferns that would have assured blessings and good fortune if used at the proper time. She'd not learn her fortune on St. John's Eve in June, but on a day much later, the eve of the first of September. For weeks, Brozek had heard troops marching west, air squadrons blocking the moon, the young men by the Gasthaus growing more violent, workers leaving the job to fight in the war.

"But St. John's is over," Mother said to him. "Long ago was St. John's. Now is September. What good is the old custom now?"

From the mirrors, he tried summoning his troops to guard the shop. He was afraid to close it for his and Fräulein Gisella's belated wreath festival. They were over two months late in observing it. What powers did September hold? he wondered.

They were to go separately, each traveling from a different place. She held his rough map drawn in pencil, the wreath, the candle. She'd never been this far on the streetcar—then to walk through the woods.

Brozek tried singing over the water as he built a fire. He'd swum so often in the deepest part that by now his reflection would surely be captured down there. The pond is accustomed to me, he thought. His fire reflected along the grassy banks. Above the screech of night birds, he said to himself, "Let us celebrate, with its old accustomed state, the Eve of St. John's." From a long way off, she watched.

Then Fräulein Gisella, who'd prepared her wreath and who now was sitting at water's edge where Brozek neither heard nor saw her, drew a match, struck it, lit the candle atop her wreath of flowers and grass. She pushed it into the pond. It floated a good way out, Brozek eagerly watching its course. All around, he heard the night screech of birds, then an owl. The deepest part of the pool reflected the candle's light.

He felt a breeze from the land.

"Brozek," she was calling. "Brozek, it's not my fault. God help me, I want the wreath to come toward you as the custom says."

He stood on the shore, the wreath drifting away.

"It's not my fault," she said.

Brozek entered the water, still warm from the hot summer. The wreath of wildflowers drifted at the whim of the breeze. Now what he saw and heard in the air was neither the smoke of St. John's Eve, which is said to bring good fortune to the harvest, nor the voices of animals talking to each other in human voices, which is said to happen on St. John's Eve. Along the Western Front, it had begun to hail. Fräulein Helsel's wreath of flowers moved further from Pan Brozek, who was to his waist in the pond. "Auguries of marriage are made on this night, my son," his mother had told him.

Along the bank, he saw dark linden trees among the pines. The sky blazed with lightning.

"Janusz," Fräulein Gisella cried.

The whole center of the pond was dark. He heard the flight of birds. The wind came up fiercely and extinguished the candle.

Fräulein Gisella ran down a path from the fierce, hot night. "It's not my fault," she called.

"Brozek, Brozek!" the shopkeeper said to himself. "What a foolish man!" He stared at his reflection on the water. The harder his breaths, the more the face broke apart.

In the sky, air squadrons passed. His reflected armies were doubtless charging forth in the dressing mirrors at home, he thought. How bravely they'd charge out to meet the invaders.

He swam toward the center where he dove down into the water looking for himself. He was halfway home. In the days before Fräulein Helsel had come into his life, he'd sat staring through a shop window. Now he was halfway through the window and the mirrors. His face and side hurt. There was nobody in the world for him. He wasn't himself. His country of mirrors was falling. He'd be alone. He'd drown alone, he thought. He touched the sand on the bottom of the pond and stayed along the bottom.

The wind came up in the town where Mother waited for him. On the door of his shop, the AUSVERKAUF sign swayed from side to side. The fierce wind came in through the window which, on the eve of the first, had been broken in his absence.

THE SIX PURPOSES OF DRILL

"Why are you eyeballing me?" Staff Sergeant Welch asks when I want to leave the drill field.

Finding a place midway between the back of his campaign hat and the historic buildings of the arcade, I say, "Sir, there's been an accident."

"Get away from me."

"Aye, aye, Sir."

In the distance, platoons practice close order drill. Carrying an M-14, I jog across the parade ground to the head.

A first lieutenant in garrison cap and summer service uniform asks, "What's wrong, Recruit?"

"Sir, the private's stomach's upset."

When I'm three paces behind the gunnery sergeant I come up to next, I say, "By your leave, Sir!"

"You stink."

"Yes, Sir. I know, Sir."

Through the frosted glass windows tilted open, the sun throws patterns across the latrine floor. For the first time since arriving in San Diego, I'm alone. A Marlboro would taste good, but at what price if I'm caught smoking without permission? On the parade ground, the platoon drills under the gaze of Corporal George, Sergeant Gribben, and Staff Sergeant Welch. The latter is bitter-eyed and red-faced. Broken blood vessels wander about his swollen nose. Sometimes he pushes his campaign hat back on his head to wipe his face with a handkerchief. Despite his cigar smoking and slight paunch, on long runs through the canyons he can stay with his recruits.

When Platoon 146 returns from the drill field, what's called "the Grinder," Staff Sergeant Welch says to me, "Diapers are not part of your basic clothing issue, Bronkowski. At the next pay call, Corporal George will accompany you to the Recruit Exchange to shop for utility trousers and skivvies to replace the ones you've tossed. Get out of my sight."

In Korea, he'd seen men have accidents. Who can blame Marines for things that happen in war? Then I come along, blond-haired, shiny-faced, soft-bellied, to shower and pamper my body. Disgusted with me and with the platoon, Staff Sergeant Welch barks something to Sergeant Gribben, the junior drill instructor. "Fall in!" Gribben says.

"Sir, yes, Sir," we say.

From its holder by the hatch, Private Dillon grabs the guidon. The red pennant at the end of a staff identifies our platoon by number. To win streamers for the guidon for marksmanship, drill, physical readiness, academics, and other skills, we compete against three platoons in the training series.

"Dress right, Dress!" Gribben says.

In short sidesteps, I move right till Private Munn's fingertips touch my shoulders and my fingertips touch Private Kieser's shoulders when he moves right. At Sergeant Gribben's next command, we drop our arms to resume the position of attention. Page 102, *Guidebook for Marines*, lists six purposes of drill: 1) "To teach discipline by instilling habits of precision and automatic response to orders," 2) "To move a unit from one place to another in a standard, orderly manner ..."

"Right face," Gribben says. We turn smartly. Page 103 defines "Snap" as "immediate and smart execution of movement." If we follow orders, perhaps the smoking lamp will be lit after chow.

When Dillon raises the guidon, we step out. Gribben is calling cadence. The DIs make Private Page a foghorn. Back and forth in front of us, Page dashes about. At 1130 hours, the human foghorn bellows like he's off the coast of Maine.

"Let that foghorn sound come from deep in your diaphragm, Page. 'Ah-hoo! Ah-hoo!' Make it low. Make it nasty. Platoon 146 does not want to collide with some pussy platoon," Sergeant Gribben is saying. "We're not pussies. We're squared away."

"Ah-hoo!" Page calls.

"That's right. Sound off so no one gets in our way. Private Kieser, don't slouch. Private Clark, why must you ditty-bop? Huber, Huber, Huber, what am I to do with a screwup like you?"

The boot heels of three DIs and sixty-one recruits hit the deck in unison. A third purpose of drill is "To improve morale by developing team spirit." "Owr, owr, owr, hedalep, hedalep" goes the cadence. We're aligned. We're squared away. If it could stay this way, if a problem didn't annoy Staff Sergeant Welch, then training could be easier, but someone—Huber? Ramage? Launderville? Page?—someone has done a terrible thing.

Now I wonder whether the smoking lamp will ever be lit. On the way to the mess hall, I imagine Gribben saying it's because of me the lamp is out.

My girlfriend encouraged me to smoke after she started. Blame her! If she tries to hide gum, candy, or other items of what the drill instructors call pogey bait when she writes me from home, the DIs will pummel me. They'll order me to swallow a gum wrapper. If I can't, they'll have me chew a stick of gum before the platoon. Another recruit in our platoon enjoyed contraband this way. After "Taps," with lights out, we tossed a blanket over him and beat him. On the eighteenth or nineteenth days of boot camp, the DIs went apeshit that someone had almost gotten away with his pogey bait. "You'll never crave pap food, will you, Recruits?" "No, Sir." "*Will* you?" "No, Sir," we yelled.

Let civilians enjoy pogey bait. Now on the thirtieth day of recruit training, July 1964, someone could offer me a California burger and I'd refuse. I'll be tough when I leave the Marine Corps Recruit Depot in September. I'll have learned hand-to-hand combat, the nomenclature of the M-14, how to parry and thrust with the fixed bayonet, even the six purposes of drill, though the last three are for NCOs.

At 1200 hours, Gribben marches us to the mess hall. He says, "No playing grab ass. No talking. You have twelve minutes. At my command, I want sixty-one hairy assholes hitting the benches in unison."

Because of the summer bug I've caught, I don't put much on the mess tray. I want to slip Private Huber a slice of bread, but I'll be in a world of hurt if I do. Huber must lose weight. In eleven minutes, fifty-nine seconds, we're outside forming around the guidon for the march back to the platoon area.

While we were away, Sergeant Campos has come aboard to relieve Sergeant Gribben. Below the shaped crown of his campaign hat is a black eagle, globe, and anchor. The shirt front buttons of his utility uniform align with his trousers' fly. Everything is freshly starched and pressed. His boots are spit-shined. The ice plant problem troubles him. Dark green, four inches tall, ice plant surrounds the Quonset huts. Some ditty-bopper has stepped on it. The damage to the three ice plant blades is irreversible, catastrophic, earth-shattering. "In five minutes," Sergeant Campos says, "I want one hundred dead flies in your grubby hands. Gnats and fleas do not count, Dippies. Do you understand? Private Markwood, bring the DI's chair from the duty hut. There *will* be no lollygagging. You've disappointed your DIs. Page, start the foghorn. Quickly. Get it done. When I say 'Time,' you maggots line up with your flies."

The platoon searches inside and outside the squad bays. Private Quinn bumps into Private Hedstrom. Floyd Settles sees a fly on a hand pump. "Where?" asks LaRoche. "There. No, it's flown over there." Ulom has one, Velarde two. On the bulkhead inside the Quonset hut, Elroy Williams zeroes in on a juicy fly. Cooper reaches up the bulkhead. A regular Venus flytrap, Velarde claims he has three now. "Ahoo, Ahoo!"

"Page, cease with that alarm," Sergeant Campos says, relaxing in his chair.

The platoon scrambles into line.

In the past day, Private Lee, whose rifle was found with a speck of rust, has had to bury the M-14 outside a Quonset hut, placing an R.I.P. sign over it. Private Draper has had to guard the Quonset huts from enemy submarines. When the DIs say things like "Up your giggy with a wawa brush," the words make no sense. Fly patrol is mindless, insane.

"How many captured?" Sergeant Campos asks.

"Sir, two, Sir," Wangler says.

"How many, Borsom?"

"Four, Sir."

"Do not give your flies to other recruits. We will extend the flies a proper burial."

When he's examined thirty-six flies, Campos focuses on Private Ramage. "I've seen this fly. It was the second one through the line. Do you think your DI is blind?"

"No, Sir, it's a new kill, Sir."

"I recognize it. Flies, like civilians, are unsanitary. You must discourage them from your presence. Get in formation. All of you. One hundred squat thrusts. Ready, exercise. One, two—" Sergeant Campos loses count. "Start over," he says as Staff Sergeant Welch and Corporal George hover about.

We bring our elbows to our knees. We place our palms on the hot asphalt. Arms stiff, we thrust our legs backward, keeping toes straight, heels up. Returning to the squat position, we go back to standing. We repeat the process, repeat it and repeat it.

When I look over, the platoon fatty boy is picking up flies. He's getting worse. The starving Huber isn't a good recruit; Ramage isn't either.

If Private Huber doesn't lose weight, he's destined for Motivation Platoon. This is where the Unmotivated go, the fatty cakes who sometimes enlist in the Marines. When Huber takes a slice of bread or a pat of butter in the chow line, the DIs remove it from his tray. He lacks esprit de corps.

The fatboy Huber and the fly thief Ramage upset the DIs. ("I've seen this fly. It was the second one through the line. Do you think

35

your DI is blind?") I upset the DIs, too. Now Sergeant Campos has a fly up his ass. "Someone's stepped on the ice plant," he says. "Do you Numbies see right here where the tips of three blades are broken? I want no diddledicking. Who did this?"

After "Taps" one night, the private in the rack above me tossed and turned because of Settles's snoring, Bertilson's and Ramage's whispering to themselves, and Huber's quiet sobbing. Maybe he was talking in his sleep when he said, "Bless me, Father, for I have sinned. I have broken the precious goddamned ice plant."

Dillon has pinned the destruction on Huber. For all the things Huber's screwed up, he's *not* stepped on the ice plant. Now the platoon is out to get him. Dillon's suspicions have been relayed to the DIs. If his life depended on it, Huber couldn't execute the vertical climb on the obstacle course, couldn't execute the "By the right flank, March" command on the drill field. Now this.

Corporal George asks, "Are you a plant lover, Huber? Were you a botany major before you washed out of that tenth-rate college?"

Brim of his brown felt campaign hat touching the front of Huber's green cloth utility cover, Staff Sergeant Welch asks, "Fatty Cakes, are you rebelling against discipline?"

We knew the end was near when poor Huber couldn't recite the sixth General Order. He stands there confused.

"Your DI doesn't speak English? Is that what's wrong that you can't understand? Do you want me to speak Esperanto? We're having great trouble with you."

"Yes, Sir," Private Huber agrees.

"No shit," Staff Sergeant Welch says. One way or another he's getting the truth. "Look what you've done. It's not *my* ice plant, Huber. It's the platoon's, the Marine Corps'. Stand still! Do you have the St. Vitus's Dance that you're moving about? You'll move when you get to Motivation Platoon, all right. Your drill instructor, who froze hands, feet, and dick at Inchon, leaving the latter permanently erect, does not fail his recruits, but he's done so this day. You'll be sent back for training."

"Sir, it wasn't him," Private Launderville says. All through boot camp, he's been quiet. "Look at him. He's helpless. *I* did it, Sir. It was accidental."

"Out of the way," Corporal George yells. Pushing aside recruits, he's over Launderville like stink on shit. "Stand at attention!" On the other side of the platoon, Staff Sergeant Welch is yelling at Huber. "We're sending your sorry ass out of here." Huber's legs are shaking.

"One for the Corps, two for the Corps—" the platoon says, doing push-ups as punishment for Huber's mistakes and Launderville's confession.

"Sound off!"

"*I* did it. I smashed three blades of ice plant," Launderville keeps saying.

"Louder!" Corporal George says to the platoon. "Louder, louder!" drowning him out. "One for the Corps, two for the Corps."

A flight is leaving Lindbergh Field. A platoon is heading on a long run. I think of how my girlfriend is preparing to write me. No pogey bait, I've told her, but she's angry about what I said the night before I left. I had to get away from home. I was going to love the Marines, I said. It made her jealous.

Who knows what she'll put in an envelope for the DIs to find? The smoking lamp might be out again. The ocean breeze has stopped. Private Norman has joined Private Page. Two foghorns run about at 1400 hours on a clear day yelling "Ah-hoo! Ah-hoo!" Ramage must do extra push-ups for lying about a fly when he didn't lie. Private Launderville is doing squat thrusts for telling the truth when he should've lied. Starved, Huber looks for flies as I say to Staff Sergeant Welch, "Sir, the private requests permission to—"

"You went to the head a few hours ago."

"Yes, Sir, the private knows this, Sir."

"Up your giggy. Get back in line. Finish your squat thrusts, Bronkowski."

"Twenty-nine for the Corps," the recruits are saying.

If I look Staff Sergeant Welch in the eye, he won't recognize me. To him, I'm not human. When I formulate a thought as Huber falls apart, I locate a place midway between the back of Sergeant Welch's campaign hat and the Quonset huts. Focused on the in-between place, I say, "Sir, Private Bronkowski's had another accident because of his summer bug, Sir."

When he yells, "Get away from me. Get away from here," I don't move. I say, "The private is sick. The private is going to have another accident, Sir," until finally a DI listens to me about Huber the fly eater, about Page the foghorn, about Ramage the liar, about all of us, and how, after the first weeks of boot camp, the fog is descending on an otherwise clear afternoon in San Diego.

PROSPECTS

The heart-breaking story of Eddie Bronkowski, heavyweight, begins here. To renew a boxing license in Wisconsin, you list a prospect's won-loss record on the application, attach his medical exam report, and say whether he's needed "an EEG, CAT scan, or MRI before being permitted to box again." If he hasn't fought professionally, you provide information relating to his training and conditioning.

At his storefront gym, Butch Maeder, a sloppy guy who couldn't dance and drove a rusted-out van, filled in the form for Edward Bronkowski.

"What's your age?"

"Twenty-four."

"Weight?"

"Two hundred five."

"Look at question six," Butch told the prospect. "'How many times has boxer'—that's you, Eddie—'been *knocked out* as a result of head blows during a bout or received *hard blows* to the head making the boxer defenseless or incapable of continuing a bout?'"

"I've had so many amateur fights that I can't recall," the Bronko answered.

Shoulders slumped, hands between his knees, he fiddled with the mouthpiece Butch Maeder had bought him.

"I'm glad you can't remember. It wouldn't look good to write this down. You bring me your license application fee, I send the application in to the Department of Regulation and Licensing, and I think we're in business."

"I've already taken the license money from my ma's purse. I'll repay her when I beat up this guy. That's how much I want to fight him and turn pro. What's my opponent's name? Val or Hal something? Hal the Gal? My Gal Hal? Ha-ha-ha."

"I like your attitude, kid. I like the cost here. Thanks to our state, it's been $5 for as long as I remember. Just think, you'll soon be a professional boxer," Butch said, always hopeful.

Three weeks later, on January 30, 1987, after being knocked out by "Pretty Boy" Valentine Hammer, Blooming Prairie, Minnesota, Ed Bronkowski wished he hadn't paid Butch the fee. With his fight purse spent getting the cut over his eye sutured ($40), his nose straightened by a doctor ($30), and Butch paid his share of the take ($40 plus the $2.50 for the mouthpiece), the Bronko had $7.50 left and faced a 150-mile drive home from St. Paul.

"That's what I got to take out my girl on, Butch, my $7.50 fight purse. I make $120 and look what I'm down to—$2."

"It's $2.50. Don't worry. You drive, and I'll buy you a cinnamon bun on the way home. Don't look in the mirror until the facial swelling goes down."

"After all my amateur bouts, I last nine minutes as a pro. What am I gonna tell my girlfriend when she sees the condition of my face? She don't know I box."

"Wear a bonnet. Wear a babushka to mass. That'll fool her," Butch quipped.

This was the Butch Maeder people knew, a sixty-year-old wiseacre with varicose veins and an Eddie Bronkowski problem. The Bronko wasn't "right," didn't have it "together," as young people said. Butch had known him a long time. A nice kid, thought Butch, but he questioned everything. As a result, it took the Bronko forever to learn certain concepts—like how, when your opponent's circling to move away from your power punch, you hook his leg to tangle him up. Such complex ideas tangled up the kid who was one *Big* question.

"Isn't that tripping, Butch?" he'd asked during the instruction.

"Don't let the ref see."

"I get warned the first time he catches me. The second time I get points taken off, right?"

"Easy, kid. This is life or death, remember," Butch said.

The way his fighter approached the manly art was the way he, Butch, approached dancing. When his wife bugged him to do the Mashed Potato, a dance from the 1960s, he couldn't make his body work. "Just feel the beat, Butch. Let yourself give in to it," Muriel would say, Butch feeling like a sissy wiggling about. "What do I do with my legs? What do I do with my arms?" he'd wonder, getting tangled up. Because he loved Muriel, who deserved some joy in life, he endured her foolishness the way he endured training Ed Bronkowski.

"Here's a trick," Butch had told him a week before the My Gal Hal fight. "Use the laces of your gloves. Rake his face. Don't let the ref see."

"Shouldn't I be ashamed of that?"

"Ashamed is when you're brain dead from a right hook, the ref signals you to a neutral corner, and you head to the blue corner. No matter what happens in the Val Hammer bout, you walk like a man. When you're champ, we'll make it your theme song. You never heard the song? Frankie Valli and the Four Seasons: *Walk like a man, talk like a man, walk like a man, my son. No woman's worth crawlin' on the earth. So walk like a man, my son.*"

Butch sang the oo-wee-oo part.

The night of the Val Hammer bout, Mrs. Bronkowski knew it was her Eddie coming in by the way he rattled the storm door. She kept it hooked when her husband and Alphonse, her older boy, the ex-Marine, were working and Ed was out. The heavy inside door to the back porch she locked when no one else would be coming home. Opening both doors, she looked for Ed among the stars. Next door, the Slinkers' house was dark except for one light on upstairs. "Eddie, should I warm up some beef noodle soup?"

"Nah, Ma," he said from the corner of the house facing the garage. He was kicking ice from the downspout.

"Don't bother Mr. Slinker with that banging. He's probably writing his short stories. Don't slip on the stairs."

"You're right," he said, handing her the remains of a cinnamon bun. "I don't feel like beef noodle."

"How was the fight? "

"Terrific," he said, tossing his coat on the kitchen chair. "When I got hit in the head, I began thinking I was in the wrong place. In forty amateur fights, I was never belted so hard. Sorry the frosting's missing off the cinnamon bun. Butch ate it with his fingers. 'Use the knife,' I told him. He'd asked the waitress for a bag of ice. When Butch thought I couldn't see him because of the swelling I was holding the ice to, his fat fingers started after the frosting."

"Don't worry. I've got news. Your girl called. When are your dad and me going to meet her? You better contact her tomorrow morning. When your dad's home from the night shift and trying to sleep, he likes the phone kept off. He don't want no one talking or calling on it. You should respect your father."

"I do. I'm sore. I'm in a low place in life. I never told my girlfriend what I do for work."

"There's no shame in it, Eddie, I mean being in the low place. We've been there."

Not like this, he said on the way upstairs.

When he got in bed, he thought of the Prom Center in St. Paul, scene of the fight card. "Let's have a good, clean professional bout," the referee was saying, then Val Hammer was driving his fists into him, into Eddie Bronkowski. As Pretty Boy's corner shouted "Work the body and his head will fall," the Bronko blocked punches, he slipped others; yet, after three three-minute rounds, the old guy's punch count topped ninety to the Bronko's ten or twelve.

"Keep your jab straight," Butch kept yelling. What jab? the Bronko had wondered during the three rounds he'd stayed upright trying to clinch with his opponent. When the first preliminary ended, people were just coming in, buying beers, looking for their seats. Talking to the fans, the promoter hurried about. It was 7:15. The main event started in three hours. Not long after, Butch would be ordering pastries at Tobie's Restaurant in Hinckley.

The Bronko remembered the ref signaling TKO, remembered Butch wiping him down with a towel, Butch with the spit bucket, Butch on the ring apron helping him negotiate the stairs. Later, with his manager on the three-hour drive home up Interstate 35, the Bronko marveled at the airs the older man's stomach gas could play.

Now the Bronko recognized the ceiling tiles in his bedroom. "I know where I am," he said. He heard his old man moving in the kitchen. "Hail to the Champ," Mr. Bronkowski said when Ed came downstairs.

"I'm going to five o'clock mass this afternoon. I've gotta use the phone after breakfast."

"Your face looks like the pu pu platter at Joe's Pagoda," Mr. Bronkowski said.

"Maybe so," Ed said.

"Take our collection envelope, Eddie. I can't attend mass when my asthma gets bad," Mrs. Bronkowski said.

The envelope went in the basket two ushers passed around during the offertory. On it was the Bronkowskis' name and today's date.

"You going to church, Pa?"

"He just got home, Ed. Tonight he has to work again."

The old man poured coffee from his cup and drank it from the saucer in the old country way. "'Who rises early, to him God gives,'" he said before he shook his head, rose from the table, and went to bed. "Two things I want," he added on the way out, "that my boy go to mass and that he pay his Polish Club dues."

"Use the phone before he falls asleep. Hurry. What's the number? I'll dial," said Mrs. Bronkowski, guiding her son by the sleeve of his bathrobe. He'd stashed the collection envelope in one of the pockets.

"Is this 398-5663?" he said. "Adele? Is that you? I didn't call too early, did I? It's 8 a.m."

"If you go to five o'clock mass, I want to show you something," she said.

"You won't recognize me."

"You're a stranger anyway."

"I'm warning you. I had a serious face-lift. You'll see. I'll sit near the side altar by the stained-glass window that says, 'Donated by the Polish Women of the Parish.'"

"Cut it short," Mrs. Bronkowski was saying, pointing to her husband's bedroom.

When Adele hung up, he said, "I'll take an aspirin and rest. I'll have the beef noodle soup later."

"I don't like that boxing game," Mrs. Bronkowski said.

"I do it for the money. I made $2.50 last night. Now I want to go back to sleep."

A few hours later, when he'd accidentally brushed his finger over his eyelashes, even they hurt. "I'm getting up, Ma," he said, wondering whether she was dusting and cleaning upstairs. He didn't hear anything from the other rooms. When the old man worked nights, he slept till three, puttered around the house, then had supper before reading the paper and taking a nap. Ed hoped the old man had gone to K-Mart.

When he saw him in the kitchen, he knew his pa hadn't slept much. A patch of gray-black hair stuck out on the side of his head. He was flexing his fingers to see how bad his arthritis felt. "You gonna shave before church?" Mr. Bronkowski asked. When Eddie said, "My face is too sore," the old man said something else. He tapped his arthritic fingers on the table to show how his son had hurt him every day of the old man's life.

At 5:20, head and body aching, the Bronko took a collection envelope from the pew in church. "I left my folks' envelope at home," he wrote, signed the envelope, and placed it in the offertory basket. With his last $2.50 heading to the church's bank account, he realized he couldn't take out his dream girl.

During communion, barely able to open his mouth to receive the Eucharist, he said "Amen," turned from the railing, and saw her. "Shame on you," she said. When he got to the pew, he covered his face. "Lord, I'm not worthy that Thou shouldst come under my roof," he prayed, hoping that she'd leave and not comment on his miserable face again. But the whole time he asked for this, she knelt two pews behind him. When mass was over, she looked angrier than ever. "You're right. I *don't* know you," she said.

"I can't see. Will you take my arm and walk me home?"

"What you do for a living can't be healthy."

"I'm zero and one. I went to confession last week. I confessed what we've been doing. I have a lot to confess."

"Do you know why I called you?" she asked, leading him out of the church. "I have ashes in this plastic bag. I took the dried palm my family keeps beside the crucifix on the wall, burned it in my parents' hibachi, and collected the ashes. I'm pregnant," she said as the wind off the lake picked up. "Who's that now?" she asked, pointing down Fourth Street past Stasiaks' house to the tracks.

"Your mother-in-law," Ed said.

"Why didn't you tell me we were meeting? I'd have fixed myself up."

Over her housedress, Mrs. Bronkowski had thrown a winter coat. Because of her asthma, in the cold air she took it slow, stopping to use her inhaler. It seemed like forever between when Ed let his girlfriend place a thumbprint of ashes on his forehead and when Mrs. Bronkowski arrived.

"We forgot the church envelope, Eddie," she said.

"This is Adele," he said.

"What are the ashes for?" Mrs. Bronkowski inquired, wheezing as her son placed his finger into the plastic bag. Not knowing what else to do, he made the Sign of the Cross on his girlfriend's forehead.

"It's a burnt-up palm from last Palm Sunday. Let me give you some," he said to his mother.

The three were passing where the creek winds to the bay through a culvert beneath Fourth Street when Butch drove up. "You don't need to pay for the mouthpiece, kid," he said.

"You been drinking, Butch? Is that beer in the back seat? You're violating the open container law. Can I have one for my walk home?

45

It'll be in honor of last night in St. Paul. Adele and me have news. Here, Ma. Here, Butch and Muriel. 'Remember that thou art dust, and unto dust thou shalt return,'" Ed said, placing ashes on their foreheads.

"We're not Catholic," Muriel said, sounding drunk. "What do we want this for?"

"Everyone has things to be embarrassed of," said the Bronko. "Don't you make Butch do the Boogaloo and the Shing-a-Ling? He told me he feels stupid dancing. This can remind you we're made of dust. Tell them the news, Adele."

"Wait till we get to your house. Your ma might want to sit down," Adele said.

"I know what it is," said Mrs. Bronkowski, taking a puff of mist from her inhaler when the news sank in about her son and his pregnant girlfriend.

"Maybe you better double *my* ash allotment," the Bronko said.

"With only one Palm Sunday palm to work with, I added other stuff from the bottom of the hibachi. I'll give *you* more ashes for sure, Ed. You deserve a lot more than your poor ma or me. I should cover your face with ashes. I should make you quit boxing and get a job at the coal dock or the ore dock."

"Ouch!" Ed said when she touched her finger to his head. "Bring the beer, Butchie. Your prospect's gonna lose his physical conditioning. My girlfriend's having a kid, she's angry at me, and I'm jobless, except I'm an up-and-comer in the ring. That's something to celebrate."

"You're a prospect. Just don't think so much," Butch said.

"Who are these people with marks on their foreheads?" inquired Mr. Bronkowski when he came downstairs from resting. "You, too?" he said when he saw his wife's forehead.

"We saved you your ashes, Frank. They smell like kielbasa," Mrs. Bronkowski said, treating herself to another puff of mist from the inhaler. "He suffers at his job," she said to Adele. "Frank don't feel good because his arthritis bothers him. To top it off, he worries about his son. You should see him worry."

This was news to Ed. Then Frank Bronkowski had ashes on *his* forehead.

No one spoke afterward. Three of the revelers—Adele, Mrs. Bronkowski, and the Bronko—knew, if they thought about it, that the true sorrow of the liturgical year began with Jesus' forty-day fast in the desert. Later, during Holy Week, the church altar would be adorned in black, Adele would worry about the baby, and Mrs. Bronkowski would worry about Eddie's not having work, which meant Adele and him would probably live at their house while Mr. Bronkowski went to the never-ending night shifts. "Who rises early, to him God gives," Mr. Bronkowski muttered as he looked to see what his wife had packed in his lunch bucket.

When Lent arrived, Eddie "the Bronko" Bronkowski would make the Sign of the Cross before training for his next fight. With the future looking bright for him, there was his pain to consider. Thankfully, the way he felt tonight, Lent was a few weeks away. Before then, he had questions—about who he'd fight next, about what Adele's folks would think of him as a son-in-law, about whether to name the baby Stanisław, Tadeusz, or maybe just plain Frank like his father. If it was a girl, her name would be Franceszka Bronkowska. Whether boy or girl, they'd honor the old man. That's what the name would be, Frank or Frances, the Bronko thought. If the commandment says "Honor Your Parents," you do just that.

Staring across at his father, Eddie Bronkowski saw, staring back, the face of a man with a losing record in life, but now that the baby's name would honor him, maybe everyone's luck would change for the better, especially Frank Bronkowski's. Then the old man was muttering as though in pain from his arthritis and whatever else had happened to him since getting up from his nap. He looked crossly at his wife. "How long we been married?" he asked.

"Serce tam rośnie—" Mrs. Bronkowski replied, repeating the words as though for the first time she understood the meaning of the saying, "The heart swells where peace reigns." "You say it, Frank."

"The heart swells—" he tried, but he was only a laborer who hadn't slept well.

"Say the whole thing like you believe in Eddie and Adele's future."

"The heart swells where peace reigns," Mr. Bronkowski said, muttering something below his breath. She thought he said, was certain he said, "Dobra żona, mężowi korona . . . A good wife is a man's crown."

"I'm glad you feel that way," Mrs. Bronkowski replied; and for a time, for a few hours, at least, everyone—the arthritic laborer, the future mother-in-law with her inhaler, the boxer, his girlfriend—all of them were as happy as could be before Lent.

Maybe you could put it this way: Wszędzie dobrze, ale w domu najlepie. In his broken English and without irony, the old man, who'd been a cavalry soldier in World War Two, would say it means, "Everywhere is fine, but it's best at home." Or maybe there *is* irony here, for everywhere is not fine in the world or at home. The old man knew this better than most.

Now Eddie would learn it, his Eddie, the one they already called "the Bum" and "the Loser" after only one pro fight.

PORT OF MILWAUKEE

Without a Transportation Worker's Identification Card, a TWIC, Leon must stop at the no trespassing signs. Seeing his headlights from the deck of the *Henry L. Stimson*, I climb down the portside ladder and hurry to meet him. The *Stimson*, a Great Lakes freighter, has wintered at Jones Island in the Port of Milwaukee. In March, we're fitting out for the shipping season.

With Leon's headlights illuminating the ice in the slip, I throw a few punches. I bob and weave to show him how classy I was. "*Zimno*," I say, when he reaches over to open the door for me. I know the word for "cold," but I don't know many others, which is why my cousin Leon's come for me. We'll go to a restaurant for him to teach me about myself before my brain goes dead and I can't learn any more.

"We'll eat, drink, and toast our ancestors," the big city insurance agent tells me. He returns home each summer to visit Grandma, my uncle Pete, Ma, me. When he's there, he fusses about everything. What does the town have to offer him, after all? It's a broken place of beat-up dreams, beat-up taverns, and empty lots the north wind blows through. Superior is bad weather, a shipyard, a coal dock, an oil refinery. Leon escaped when he was twenty-three.

Despite the bleakness of my hometown, most winters when the lakes freeze and shipping ends, I stay up there. When I take time off during shipping season, I also head north to see my mother, Evelyn Bronkowski. She says nothing about the heartaches I cause her until Leon in his Honda CR-V makes his annual jaunt north. Then she starts in, "Eddie, study for your oiler's license. Your cousin Leon had no advantages. He was an insurance salesman. Now he's a vice president. Why not advance yourself?"

"I was smart like him once. Remember, Ma? I attended college for a month. I was gonna be a psych major." She never answers because there's no more to say on the subject.

Last week before I left home, she bought me a jacket with zippered pockets and a zippered lining. In the new, blue, zippered jacket, I still look like Eddie Bronkowski, the pug with a face he can't escape. Whereas Leon dresses in black, which he claims is the German style of fashion, I'm in this jacket with the zip-on hood waiting for my boat to fit out and shipping season to begin.

"I got these scar tissues when I lost a split decision here at the Mecca," I tell Leon. "I lost a TKO to a bum in Green Bay, too. I was five and twenty as a pro."

This is what I don't say as we drive up Lincoln Avenue. I own a blue jacket courtesy of Ma, and I have a berth on the *H.L. Stimson* one-fifth the size of my room at home. I have no favorite bar to drink in, no one to look after me. Add to this I was banged up in the ring for ten years and sometimes I'm not right in the head. I feel it happening. The names of places I've fought in like Lorrain, Ohio, Omaha, and St. Paul don't come back to me. I get nowheres when I try thinking. It's tied in with the scar tissues on my face from being cut and sewn up.

Last week, astern the *Stimson*, I watched a Coast Guard cutter break the harbor ice. We'll soon pass beneath the Hoan Bridge into the brash of Lake Michigan (ice that's broken and jumbled like my brain), and when we do, and when we load cargo in Escanaba, Two Harbors, or someplace, I will grow lonely facing another season on the lakes. I'll wash the deck with high pressure hoses, lug mooring cables along docks, slip them over spiles. The problem is we haul nothing to heal a man's soul. The same age as my cousin, forty-five, I'll never advance beyond deckhand status or get back in the ring. That leaves me Leon and no one else tonight.

"In this joint we're going to, I'll introduce you as the guy from Beer Belly Boulevard and Knockout Lane who doesn't know if it's Easter Monday or the Fourth of July. It's scar *tissue*, by the way. Can't you get it straight?"

"I'll get it perfect," I tell him. "I earned this nose. Willy Polite smashed it again when I was thirty. My cheekbones are swollen. I got scar tissues on my face and heart from people laughing at me. Scar tissue. Scar tissues. Does my description match the face you see?"

I don't mind his teasing me. He's succeeded in business by being tough. I'm tough, too. I can take a wallop like I can take a run-down neighborhood in a big city. Sometimes I forget what Leon remembers for me, like certain dates and who I fought and when my wife left me.

"Welcome," he says when we get to the tavern, our first refreshment stop. Out the car window are broken beer and wine bottles. When Leon opens the door of the tavern, everyone stares at us.

"This ain't right. You must've taken a wrong turn," I say.

On a battery-operated chair like my ma uses to get around the supermarket back home, a sign says something in Spanish. There are other words and directions I don't understand.

"It's changed a little. Two bottles of Piwo Okocimskie for those who speak our language," Leon tells the lady bartender.

"No Polish beer," she says.

"Where's the polka band?" Leon asks to *something*, maybe the old owner's spirit. "What happened here? A year back this was Polish. Who belongs to the cart?" he asks.

"My son," she says.

She has olive-colored skin. She tells us that on their way to the U.S., her son got hurt. She limps when rain's coming, she says, but her son limps all the time. A store donated the cart for his use.

"Your kid banged up that bad?" I ask.

"You, too, señor? You have my sympathy."

"The Sweet Science," I say. "My cousin's showing me what it was like here when this was Polish."

"Sure, I'm showing you," he says. "Look at the poster for the mariachi band—Ramón Ayala y los Bravos del Norte. The Pabst Blue Ribbon display is new, too. See? It's a timer's bell from a boxing match hanging there. When you want a beer, you pull the chain on the bell to signal 'PBR Me ASAP. Time for Another Round.'"

If Leon rang it, I'd keep my chin down. I'd pound an opponent's body till the bum dropped his hands. Everyone would laugh at my putting on a show, but for one night in a bar called La Tequila, formerly the Polonia Tavern, I'd be the champ and the lady-bartender-señora might buy me a pickled pig's foot to honor my delusions.

Then I'm dancing the Punch-Drunk Polka. I see the beat-up faces of a featherweight and a flyweight. Maybe they've lost more fights than me. Maybe they're from some South American country.

As I add a sixth win to my ring record, Leon interrupts my thoughts. "Why's the Black Madonna of Częstochowa hidden back there? That icon saved Poland when the Swedes invaded in the old days. When they slashed her face on the painting in the monastery at Jasna Góra, the cuts bled. Her holy image deserves the best. The Madonna doesn't belong behind the beef jerky and pigs' feet."

When the bartender brings the icon over, I see the scars on her cheek. The child in her arms wears a crown like hers. Leon kisses the picture. I've seen him act stupid many times, but he's respectful and reverent now. Who am I to judge him when his business sense has made him an executive?

"The Madonna's tears are for this big galoot," Leon says. "You bury her in there behind everything, she means nothing. It's lousy when places like the Polonia go to hell, señorita?"

"Señora," she says.

As the featherweight watches all this, the flyweight plays "Streets of Bakersfield" on the jukebox. Leon regrets the Polonia's fate more each minute. It's like his life has depended on a Polish tavern. When I look down the bar, a guy with a face hard like mine runs his finger across his throat.

"You know what a Mexican backhoe is, Eddie?" Leon asks.

"A shovel?" I say.

"When they cut weeds in a white guy's ditch, the weed whackers are called what?"

"Mexican golf clubs. You told me that one last summer back home. You're going to get your ass jumped."

But he keeps going. "What are the first three words out of a Mexican baby? 'Attention, K-Mart shoppers.'"

"When John Paul II came to Mexico, he spoke Spanish out of respect for the people. We're all children of God," I say.

When I tell him to shut up, the three guys brush past. As if to thank my cousin for insulting them, they say "*Muchas gracias*," ringing the timer's bell.

Leon lifts his beer to them. "We've got places to go, too," he tells the barmaid. "Can I borrow the Black Madonna to guard us on our sightseeing tour?"

By the time we get outside, the boxers have hurried off past empty buildings. "This was once a swell neighborhood, Ed. Immigrants built the Basilica of St. Josaphat with their own money and hard work. We had Puɫaski Park and Kościuszko Park. Now everything's behind safety gates."

"Talk about something else," I tell him. "Show me the past. Show me the old world. Let me know if I'm the loneliest guy you ever saw. I trust you."

"Our past is the flight of Polish people to the suburbs. Rudzinski's Fashion Clothes, gone. ADWOCAT law office, gone, moved out. Let's walk. Everything's boarded up. We need to clear our heads."

"My head's fine."

"Come on, keep up with me. I want to tell you something that'll clear *my* head for sure. Listen, I don't know about the old country. Anyone can read a beer bottle label and say Piwo Okocimskie when they order a beer. I don't know much else but the insurance business. I'm not a vice president. I'm an assistant to an assistant to an assistant. I might be let go of. Things aren't good at work. Look at the garbage here."

This is the great Leon of the Cream City of Milwaukee. To Ma and me, he's heroic like Kościuszko or Pułaski. I don't know what to say when he tells me he's not important.

"I was drinking when I came to get you. I tossed the empties."

"Ma and me depend on you. Can't you straighten out? Ah, I'm not reconnecting when my brain's in this condition. I know what happens when I'm going downhill. I think of my fights. I remember the Moose Hall. I'm making my hometown debut. My white T-shirt says EDDIE BRONKOWSKI in red letters Ma ironed on the night before. As I head for the ring, I see our grandma raising her rosary. A miniature Polish flag is in her other hand. She's waving it, praying for Mighty Edziu, Superior's heavyweight.

"Then it gets me. I ain't visited her in six months. I told myself I couldn't go see her because she kept the heat too high in her apartment or because the clock ticked too loud for my cauliflower ears or because nobody spoke till she piped up, 'The world's coming to an end, Eddie. Pray the rosary.'

"I'm still embarrassed about the time I fought at the Moose in front of Grandma. The hall lights went down, the announcer announced me, and I looked at her and cried. I never visit her, yet she comes to watch me. A sensitive pro with a zero and three record, by then I was hyperventilating so much that my manager shook his towel to keep the air moving. In front of three hundred people, I'm weeping when Butch tells me, 'Get the hell out and fight.' He pushes me toward the center of the ring. I duck, feint, and lay the guy out. What kind of thing was that to tell me, that I'm over-stimulated like someone getting counseled before being sent to the time-out room in grade school?"

What I tell Leon brings no pleasure. I want to slip away from these memories. Someday when no one expects it, I'll go into myself and stay there. There'll be no Superior, no Leon, no Ma. When people visit me, I'll stare at the wall.

Leon isn't listening when I start swearing. I could fill the dark with punches and never KO the things bothering me. When we get to the Kraków restaurant, a few old-country Poles are finishing their coffee.

The lights go off. The waitress motions at us through the door she's locking. She turns the sign to closed.

"Can I use the bathroom?" Leon asks. "We're out walking."

"Go in back," she says.

It's dark where she directs us. As Leon relieves himself, he says, "This Chinese couple gets engaged. They work in a restaurant, a Chinese place. Everything on the menu's numbered—"

"I don't like jokes about other countries. You know why, Leon? Because they hurt the people they're about. I'm not even from Poland, and I know what it's like. This guy on the *Stimson* gave me five pennies stuck together in a circle. He soldered the edges of each to form the circle. 'Here's a Polish nickel for you,' he said."

When Leon laughs, someone jumps the fence separating the garbage cans from the alley.

"What's going on?" he asks.

"I'm draining my enchilada," Leon says.

"He's pretty important," I say.

"This is funny . . . your 'enchilada,'" the visitor says. While I'm thinking how to tell Ma that Leon might lose his job, we're outnumbered by the guys from the tavern. There are five of them now.

"*Gracias*," the featherweight says when Leon zips his fly. "Hold on. You've heard of a baby that says 'Attention, K-Mart shoppers'? We've heard of this baby. Where is the K-Mart you spoke of? Are you going there?"

"I need Depends," Leon says. It's no laughing matter that two Polish guys might get killed. I can't protect him. I ain't boxed since the Bughouse Tavern bout in Carlton, Minnesota, where the fight was held outdoors under a big tent. It was raining. When I came to, the ring-card girl was carrying a sign advertising "Cassandra Bail Bonds." Looking worried about me, the doc waved ten fingers in my face. "How many you see?" "Eleven," I told him.

"Señors, it is not good for you to meet us?" the flyweight asks.

"We like the company of the people of the world, don't we, Ed? Did you hear about the ruptured Chinaman, Mr. One Hung Low?"

"We're in the mood for Mexican jokes only," the middleweight says. "Raphael, tell them the joke of the Mexican golf clubs. Tell them the joke of the Mexican backhoe. Do you have time to listen? Tonight is not good for your jokes? We should meet another night?"

"It smells like sauerkraut around here," I say.

"Polish aftershave," Leon says.

"You're in the wrong place, señor," the featherweight says. "The joke is on the gringos. Show us your enchiladas."

One of them walks toward me. "See?" he says. "We're going to use this on both of you. In a minute, you will each be minus two chalupas."

When the knife cuts the front of my jacket, Leon acts like *he's* been hurt. Whatever has happened to me, I ain't worried. "Worry is negative energy," my ex-wife used to say. I hear the ref's instructions, hear him tell me, "Touch gloves and come out fighting." Doing what a guy does in the ring, I throw a left. Jab, jab, right cross. Though I let him have everything in my arsenal, my fists don't connect. I hear the bells from the Bughouse Tavern and the Knockout Saloon. "I'll get to my cell phone. I'll call the cops," Leon says. I'm not thinking of him. I'm doing what a guy does in the ring.

For every punch I throw, the Mexican could have countered with fifteen more. Instead, he dances around. He knows I'm punchy. Then there's darkness in the ring, the sound of fading cheers, rounds lost. Here I am, the "Bronko" Bronkowski, slugging the hell out of a lake wind in Milwaukee because I don't notice the Mexicans have taken off. Leon's gone, too.

"The car's okay," he says when I catch up with him.

"What about my jacket?"

"You didn't protect us worth shit back there. I always heard you were a tomato can. The car's the important thing," he says, relieved that we have the Polish icon. We're two bums on a dark street. Maybe the worst is Leon.

"What if my head got injured if I was knocked down or something?" I say, telling him what I've been trying to get across for three hours.

The words let me know my brain is working, that I remember things. I say the name of every city I can think of: Oconomowoc, Rhinelander, Green Bay. "We have the highest waterfall in the state up north," I tell him. "I was in Marshfield. I was getting in roadwork. It was autumn. The air sparkled, Leon. The church bells rang." I tell him, "The time Butch, my corner man, wiped my tears with his towel, he said 'You idiot, get hold of yourself. Get out there and box.' There was another time when I was strong and beat a guy from Minot."

The more I tell Leon, the more I think it's a foreign language I'm learning, the language of the foreign country I've been traveling through. My cousin can learn nothing from me, but I don't know what other language to use. "It wasn't only for Grandma. It was for you I cried. It sure was earned back then, Leon, my crying. You left us, came down here to a big city to be important. Look what happened. Now you drink and joke about One Hung Low and Mexican babies."

"I'm glad I'm not you," he says. The way he looks at me hurts. I wanted him to connect me to something, but it ain't gonna work tonight. Ma accidentally hurts me sometimes. People on the *Stimson* hurt me like when the Polish nickel of five pennies in a circle mysteriously appears as though some crew member has it in for me. Nobody does it like Leon, though—Leon and his dumb jokes about me and about Mexicans and Chinese people.

On this last stretch of street before the Polonia, litter blows around our shoes. My eyes fill with tears as I name more places in this state where Leon would never be happy. Up north the forests and small towns take over. Up north Ma is safe in her house on Fourth Street. Grandma is safe and Uncle Pete and my nephews. In the north woods, we're safe from the embarrassments we've suffered in and out of the ring.

"Superior, Washburn, Ashland." It comes back to me that my father was born in Poland. I hope my mind is clear on that forever: He was born in northeastern Poland. I want to say this and the city names so that if the newcomers to Wisconsin hear me they'll know there were people like my pa in the Dairy State, people that worked on ore docks, coal docks, and in flour mills. I want to yell in honor of them, but I don't yell, for something nags my mind when I say: "Beloit, Wausau, Portage." I can't get past the names. I love this state. Something's changed in the Cream City, though. Leon was going to be my travel guide. Escorting me into the past, he'd show me everything. Now Poland's gone. Where are the people I came to see?

This new thing that's happened nags me till I want to shut out the words that've passed through my mind. I get nagging ideas that block other ideas. Then I don't feel good. The more the vice president looks afraid, the more I realize our white faces mean nothing when somebody in a store around here can say, "Come in, señor." This ain't bad what's happened, but I wish I could've seen how it was. Now there's nothing left of Polish Milwaukee but street names and a restaurant that's locked us out. What's happened bothers me enough that I tell my cousin, "You ain't the same, Leon."

"You never were the same. You were always screwy. People talked about you. You'd never believe what I heard—that you were stupid, that you couldn't fight as an amateur. Then your wife left you when you were losing."

"It ain't important. My job's on the boat. I take care of Ma when I'm home. That's important. I hold nothing against anyone, not like you. I ain't right. But screw you. At least I'm not a big shot on his way down."

He looks like he'll cry. He has no one beneath him in life but me. It wouldn't hurt or matter if he hit me. Nothing hurts me. When the high and mighty Leon comes toward me, he takes a swing. He pushes me, then hits me again. I don't feel it. When I try to hug him, I see his fancy black clothes. My ear swells. It's more stuff I can forget.

"Where you going?" he asks when I turn away, ears ringing from how hard he slugged me. "I'll drive you to your boat."

"I don't need a ride," I tell him.

Even if I have to leave the great Leon Adjukiewicz with all my memories, I must hurry to the safety of the *H.L. Stimson* at the dock by the water treatment plant. The ringing will end when we leave Milwaukee. Out on Lake Michigan and Lake Erie, I'll have no memory of Leon. No more embarrassment, no more beautiful ideas about

Polish neighborhoods. Leon can keep them, every memory I ever had until the bell rings and my last fight ends.

"Wait, Eddie," Leon yells, but I can hardly hear because of the ringing in my head.

"I don't know where I am," I yell to him. "I can't remember where you took me to."

Then I'm passing Kosciuszko Park on South Seventh, and I have put two or three blocks between us. Then it's a mile. Then I'm back in the country where I've been traveling and where nobody will ever find me again.

THE SECOND COOK ON THE HENRY L. STIMSON

Imagine an old, seaworthy vessel steaming into port. I work on the *Henry L. Stimson*. Call me Verna. The lonely in this wanderer's tale include Captain Randall, though we know little about the Old Man, who doesn't fraternize with us. This is as it should be since he has great responsibilities as master of the *Stimson*. However, we know he lost a daughter in an accident in Alpena, Michigan. The mate, Anders Anderson, L'Anse, Michigan, experiences sadness with each text message his wife sends. She's losing her sight and is alone during shipping season. Is it "hysterical blindness" from believing the mate will never return to her? Marcus Rossiter, bosun, Maumee, Ohio, has a daughter addicted to methamphetamine. Orville Lee, Staunton, Virginia—his marriage is failing. Others, myself included, complete the list of the sad, loveless crew.

I've changed over the years I've been aboard. My neck and chest, once white (pink when Lloyd, my husband, made me blush), are ruddy. The white food-handler's jacket exaggerates this. As I brush my hair before the mirror, I see the darkness under my eyes, the slightly sagging chin. As one of six women sailing the American side of the Great Lakes, I do what I can to look okay for the men whose lives are marked by tragedy. Bill Lamson, oiler, Herbster, Wisconsin, saw his house burn from a lightning strike. Vernon Tushar, steward, learned last week that his son was wounded by an IED in Afghanistan. Ernie Schaub's brother has congestive heart failure. When good crewmates have problems, I try to make them happy.

On this golden morning, Captain Randall radios the Aerial Lift Bridge. As we enter the Duluth piers, he sounds one long and two short blasts of the horn, "the Master's salute." The bridge tender responds. One long. Two short. Knowing my husband is performing his ritual on the west pier, the *Stimson*'s porters and stewards look out at him or smile and wave to the other tourists as we glide through the entry. Startled by the noise of the bridge-tender's horn, no doubt Lloyd will put his hands to his ears. He writes me saying he'll watch us come into port.

When six months had passed after I left him, I stayed out six more months to work on the *Stimson*. By October 2005, twelve months had passed, then fifty-four months, then sixty-one. Now it's been 2,555 days, eighty-four months, seven years, since I've looked into Lloyd Larson's hazel eyes. Seven years of smooth sailing. During this time, I've advanced to second cook. When his language drove me off, his language of no language, I'd written him the two words that were left in me, "Goodbye forever," taped the note to the dresser mirror, and caught a Yellow Cab to the waterfront.

Out on the lakes, I have people to talk to, whereas at home I knew when the eye of a storm was settling in. Lloyd would grow quiet. I'd hear low whistles followed by whispered messages to himself as though he were amazed at something. "Pss, pss, shh, sure," the whispers sounded like, then the whistle as though he'd learned something terrible about me, then his stares, sighs, silence.

Things improved when the storm passed. He had a lousy job at the fiberboard plant, and, okay, I was no longer his dream girl, but married people work things out. Not Lloyd and me, though our life together had been good. As members of the Central Assembly of God, we'd offered Christian witness to others, but when we had time off, we took the fifth wheeler to the Boundary Waters or to the Upper Peninsula of Michigan. When the Rutabaga Festival came around, we drove seventy miles to Askov, Minnesota, for a bushel basket of that tasty vegetable. During Blueberry Festival, we went to Iron River, Wisconsin. Then something happened and squall lines hit the house so hard it shook. Why wouldn't he tell me what it was? He was thirty-seven back then. The Book of Sirach, chapter 9, verse 2, says, "Give no woman power over you to trample upon your dignity." But what power? In our marriage, he'd always kept the car keys from me and controlled the bill paying. In stormy moods, he'd rip through the dresser looking for T-shirts. In his fits and rages, he wanted to say he was being suffocated by dust, but then the coughing seized him. You should have seen it. He'd hold onto the kitchen counter or bathroom sink, bend forward, and hack till he was speechless and couldn't inform me that the difficult life had gotten to him. After I left, I knew I'd been wrong to abandon my husband because of his failure with words. He hadn't known how to tell me his dirty waterfront job was killing him. That's what it was. His anger had less to do with me and everything to do with the fiberboard plant.

What would the Central Assembly of God church have done if a repentant wayfarer, after a week or a month away, returned from sailing to surprise her husband during Bible study? In my berth, realizing I'd made a mistake by leaving him, I read the Holy Book. The only bible in the Stimson's library differs from mine at home, but God's word taught me nonetheless. Tobias 4.14: "Never suffer pride to reign in thy mind, or in thy words: for from it all perdition took its beginning." Numbers 15.30: "But anyone who sins defiantly, whether he be a native or an alien, insults the Lord, and shall be cut off from among his people."

Now I'm cut off from the Assembly of God. When we're loading the Stimson, grain dust sometimes bothers me the way wood-particle dust choked Lloyd. All day the grain trimmers guide chutes over the Stimson's holds. The long chutes hang from grain elevators towering above the waterfront. We could carry fifty thousand additional bushels of wheat if we didn't have to stay more buoyant in November, December, and early January when we sail under a so-called winter-draft because of the threat of bad weather and heavy seas. To go to Buffalo and back takes seven or eight days. Preferring the watery portion of the earth, I don't step ashore in "the Queen City of the Great Lakes" or anywhere else.

On summer evenings, with the land people settling into their homes unaware a vessel is passing far out on the lake, I bring a lawn chair astern, a gift from the crew. While reading Ecclesiastes, Isaiah, or the Book of Psalms, I say the verses aloud. On the Vanity of Pleasure: "I undertook great works; I built myself houses and planted vineyards; I made gardens and parks and set out in them fruit trees of all sorts," Ecclesiastes 2.4–5. On Desire, which is also "vanity and a chase after wind," I look out at Detroit or Gary or East Chicago and read, "Who knows what is good for a man in life, the limited days of his vain life (which God has made like a shadow)? Because—who is there to tell a man what will come after him under the sun?" Ecclesiastes 6.9–12.

As I read, the sun sets with me thinking of Lloyd. Was he working? Was he keeping up his strength, eating right? It's natural to remember the man you married. Now other men cared for me. Because they've welcomed me onto the *H.L. Stimson*, I think of them a lot, though in a different way than I think of Lloyd on the pier when the *Stimson* puts in. These good men of the *Henry L. Stimson* are my family. How special Marcus is. He's redoing his kitchen in Maumee, Ohio. How dear Anders Anderson. He's restoring an old car. Butch is a reader and philosopher. Orv Lee is one of the best.

When I need more privacy, I remain in my berth. Inland seas surround me. Storm-tossed in summer, they're roiled and cursed by the stronger gales of fall, such gales as a man ashore will never understand. When I finish out a season and the *H.L. Stimson* and other vessels are berthed in the frozen ports of the Great Lakes, my isolation becomes great with the crew gone. "So long, Verna. Hope you don't freeze," they tease as they walk down the gangway. During the shipping season, I'm active among them and popular with them.

With most of them. There was one I knew a little less than the others. He was a strange one, a wordless traveler who went about his business and bothered no one. If he was hungry, he ate. If he was tired, he slept. There wasn't much more to it.

"Why are you aft here?" he asked me one day.

"I'm reading."

"What's so great that you want to read about it?"

"I'll show you. I'll read from the Gospel of Luke," I said. "Imagine this taking place on Lake Superior: 'Now it came to pass that he and his disciples got into a boat, and he said to them, "Let us cross over to the other side of the lake." And they put out to sea. But as they were sailing . . . a squall swept down upon them. So they came and woke him, saying, "Master, we are perishing." Then he arose and rebuked the wind and the raging of the water, and they ceased, and there came a calm. And he said to them, "Where is your faith?"' What if *you* were a disciple of the Lord?" I asked my shipmate when I was witnessing to him.

After the first and second sessions, one thing led to another. In the close quarters of a lake boat, you wouldn't think so much time would pass before you became acquainted with someone. We'd take turns reading, then I'd talk about what we'd read, and he'd try to understand. Proverbs 22.11: "The Lord loves the pure of heart; the man of winning speech has the king for his friend."

After a while, neither of us knew how to proceed with what we were doing. The long evenings passed. Sometimes I didn't see him. Having no practice with an emotional attraction like ours (caused by Scripture studies, you could say), I knew he felt uncomfortable. I did, too. By walking to the bow, maybe he was clearing his mind of me. Then in the crew's mess, I'd catch his eye.

When he left the *Stimson* for a week, he sent me a card. He bought me a doll. During the time we were seeking each other, our hearts at play, I breaded his pork chops. On a pad of paper, he doodled my name. He was always the sweetest man. When we looked for signs of God's presence in our love, we knew that everything had grown from that one beginning seed when he'd first walked aft to see me.

My face shiny from the heat in the galley, I must have looked terrible sometimes. Nothing about him displeased me, except he looked bewildered, as though he were trying to find a way back from where he'd been traveling. I knew he regretted what he'd done in life. The swollen ridges over his eyes proved this—old scars on a journeyman's face. The pain I saw there I could also hear in his voice. "When a guy gets hurt or doesn't want to fight, I fill in for him," he said, as though he were still boxing. Now he was a journeyman on the *H.L. Stimson* plying the Great Lakes from Duluth to Buffalo.

One night he said right out, "I think of you."

"Why?"

"I don't know. I've been away in my head."

"Shh—" I said.

When he touched my face, he said, "I didn't know how to say this."

"Now you have," I said, knowing the heart is free once it admits its truth.

But what about me? Didn't I tell him, "No more, Ed," when he stroked my hair so gently under the stars that night on the fantail? Didn't I let him hold my hand?

I wrapped coconut macaroons for him to eat after lunch. Sometimes he'd thank me then forget what he was thanking me for. "Your thoughts will return," I said. If he didn't talk, *I* did—about the appliances in the galley, about my parents, my grandparents, my high school days. "You want to know how to make an almond crème?" I asked once when he came to the fantail. "Crush almonds, scald the sweet cream—" On a paper plate, I brought him more than he could eat.

On the nights when he was thinking clearly, we talked on and on. I've done what the Holy Book forbids: "But to those who are married . . . the Lord commands that a wife is not to depart from her husband," 1 Corinthians 7.10. Then the talking was over. By walking the decks of the *H.L. Stimson*, I'd kept my body healthy. Ed's physical conditioning hadn't left him. My berth has a desk, a chair, a bed. There was room for lovers to wonder at how things happen in the world.

Satisfied, we'd watch the moon from the bow or the fantail. When I mentioned that the guys when they went ashore bought me beauty products, such as firming formulas, daily renewal creams, and White Rain shampoo, he said, "A white rain falls on cloudless nights." We forgave each other our foolishness. If I said "Round Two" after supper, it meant dessert. If I said "Round Three," he'd gently kiss my face and hold my hand, something you wouldn't expect from a deckhand and journeyman.

When the *Stimson* arrives, look for the man with the eyeglasses and graying hair. To this day, Lloyd stands on the pier in Canal Park imploring me to return. I've seen him carrying the signs he writes out his feelings on. I doubt he'll talk to you, but look at the signs.

"Why did you break up?" my shipmates ask me.

"Who?"

"You and the fellow on the pier. You're not together."

"Who's that?" I ask.

No wonder I sometimes prefer the boat when the crew leaves for winter. While they've talked and talked about themselves, I've talked little about myself. During winter layup, when we berth in port for three months, the lakes freeze, the shipping season ends. Until the "fit-out" crew returns in March to ready the vessel to sail, I'm alone, the crew gone to their joys and sorrows in Alpena and L'Anse. Bill Lamson has a granddaughter. Orville Lee finally got to see his niece perform in a skating show. Ed stays at his mother's. During this time as I paint their quarters and read the emails and letters they send, the steel hull moans and creaks. Bound by her 858-foot-long hull and 105-foot beam, I stare out at the channel markers, piers, and warehouses in the ice-bound harbor.

With no one aboard, I confess things aloud. Last January, I said, "I am in love." Who would hear after I'd gone by flashlight down the ladder into the cargo hold to check that no valves leaked? Down there deep in the belly of the *Stimson*, I sang God's praise. I heard echoes in that steel chamber. If Ed saw me in the gloom, he'd have wanted to come to me. "Out of the depths, I cry to you, O Lord!" I called from the darkness. *If I could have had my husband here, maybe I'd have forsaken the seagoing life. Maybe it wouldn't have been too late for Pastor Ron to help us. Lloyd would have said "Hallelujah." But what would we be together in, a life without life in it? From the windows of our bungalow, a gray lake would meet a gray sky. When I froze in that house, rather than turn up the heat, Lloyd would've wrapped a gray shawl around me.*

This talking got crazy in the hold. For the past five years, the *Stimson* has over-wintered at Jones Island in the Port of Milwaukee. From the pier by the water treatment plant, I could see the dome on the Wisconsin Gas building change color with the weather. I could see U.S. Bank, the clock tower landmark, Miller Brewing, the Milwaukee traffic. Back then, Lloyd Larson was making cardboard signs at our kitchen table, the table I'd once set for dinner as I struggled with my conscience. From the hold, I'd cry "Dear Jesus" as I recalled abandoning my husband.

Now it's October. The hillsides are golden. Lloyd must know I've stopped looking for him among the tourists strolling the pier. When the *Stimson* docks at the grain elevator, my husband will leave his latest plea hanging from the chain-link fence. Then he'll wait in his car for me.

"Something's bothering your guy," Les Peterson says in the galley when I'm putting pies in the oven.

"He's signaling," says Vern Tushar, hunching over his coffee.

"It's not me he's signaling."

"Who then?" Vern says.

When I bring Ed a glass of milk, I ask, "What did you see on the pier?"

"You should pay attention to your old man," Bull LaVoy interrupts us when he walks in and overhears all the talk. "It looks like something's wrong with his health." Then Bull changes the topic. "Are you making cinnamon rolls today?"

None of the sweet-eaters knows what's going on with me. So now, according to them, I should pay attention to Lloyd, my husband. "Seven years have passed, boys. I don't know why today means anything different," I say, feeling bad that they're after me because of what a man has written on cardboard. With the turbine engines roaring in the engine room below, it's hot in here. When I open the portholes, the smell of fresh paint wafts in. I'll suffocate if I don't get air.

"All I know is you should pay attention," Bull says. "You should worry about Ed's condition, too. His mind's going."

"There's baking to be done."

Twenty minutes later, it's Ed. "If you went ashore for an hour," he says, "it won't harm anything."

It's like the scheme of reuniting me with my husband has overtaken all of them. When I can't take it, I head to my berth. I can't think here, though. It's filled with memories.

"I got it," Ed says. "This was on the guy's sign. Your husband's sign. Look through the porthole or come out if you can't read it from in there."

On the slip of paper with "Allouez Marine Supply" at the bottom, Ed's written my husband's words, I'M DYING OF HEART DISEASE. DYING OF LUNG INFECTIONS. HELP ME, HELP ME, VERNA!

Lloyd doesn't mean it. Still, seven years to the day after I left him, this comes up. I'M DYING. LUNG INFECTIONS. SORROW. GREAT DESPAIR. *I* was dying once, too. On the first evening of my exile, I'd watched the deckhands secure the hatch covers, watched Captain Randall and the stewards and porters stare at the horizon where the autumn moon rose. Lloyd must be stunned by the silence, I remember thinking. I'd have bet back then that he was remembering the days we'd watched the promise of a golden moon rise above the watery horizon. Seven years ago, he'd probably whispered to himself, "Christ will come to us. Hallelujah!"

At 1730, Ed stops by. "Go," he says.

At 1815, he says, "You have to set things right. What if he dies?"

Suppose nothing's changed, suppose there'll be silence.

When Ed returns, I'm in my berth putting things together. As the guys wait for me, they observe the harvest moon. Will it help us understand our hearts? When I was young, Lloyd fooled me. He'd quoted scriptures. Now I'm reluctant to be accepted again into the Assembly of God. A few hundred feet to the gangway, thirty steps down a ladder, a quarter-mile along the dock to the guard shack—I'll not have been this close to Lloyd in years. "How are you, dear husband?" I'll ask.

"You ready?"

"No."

"The moon's rising in our honor," Ed says.

When I tell him to come in for a moment, I remember the silences of marriage, the ill-will, something in the heart that separates two people. Toward the end, I took care of Lloyd but didn't care for him.

This berth is so small I don't know how Ed and I fit in here. Objects have been blessed by us. The air itself blessed by two people once happy to let the world sail past.

"I can't leave you," I tell Ed.

"It's no good seeing him on the pier," he says. "We love you. You never brought us bad news. You have your chance now. It'll hurt us to see you go. We'd never say anything to you, but the man out there is dying. How can we keep you from him when he's sick? What happens when *I* get worse? I forget things. The guys know my mind's going."

When I ask him to look in the mirror on the bulkhead, then to decide how I should proceed, Ed's reluctant to raise his eyes. In the mirror, I've checked my appearance for so long. "Do this for me. Look at yourself," I say, but he won't look up. "I can't leave you," I tell him as I guide his face with my hands, seeing my own face reflected beside his. Finally, we look at each other in the mirror.

Reflected is the outline of a life—our faces, the photocopied menus scattered on a bunk, a wool blanket, a pair of soft-soled shoes, a hand mirror from my purse. "Don't let go of our memories," I tell him.

As I pack my things and try not to forget the doll he gave me last year, the doll that says I LUV YOU on it, Ed helps me get ready.

Outside, my dreamer guides me around the grain piles spilled on deck. Les carries my bags. I carry my purse. The men intend to send me away because another man is dying ashore. They also do it because Ed is sinking into the past. Bill, Nick, Dave, Orville, Bull—on a calm evening with a harvest moon, they can't believe winter's coming.

"What are you thinking, Ed?"

"That I'll keep you in my heart," he says.

"My kids are growing up," Les Peterson says. "I never see them."

"I'll be happy when shipping season ends," Bull says.

"Lloyd and I have no children," I say as we pass the holds where during winter layup with the crew gone I've prayed to hear a voice. "I'll miss you," I tell all of them. "You've been good to me."

"We'll come ashore. We'll walk you to the fence," the guys say.

"You don't have to," I say. "Haven't we been happy all these years out on the lake?"

"You've got to do this for your husband," they say. "Do it for Ed, too. He won't remember you. Maybe in a month he won't even be aboard."

I know that without me they'll still survive the winter-draft months. Squalls will buffet them. Sorrows on land will be made known to the captain, the first-assistant engineer, any and all of them, but they'll get by. As the vessel hauls around in towering waves, howling winds and spray will assail them. In heavy seas, a wanderer will put up the roll bar on the galley stove while I'm home safe with Lloyd. My leaving is the best thing to help Ed forget.

"Do you want to say goodbye?" he asks me.

"I can't," I say, kissing his forehead. "You'll always be in my heart. Do you remember what you told me off of Copper Harbor?"

"Was it about the white rain?"

"You remember," I say. I whisper words of such longing. Kissing him fills me with happiness again. When I touch my fingers to his face, he says "the Quentin Earl fight." When I touch his eyebrows, he says "the Willy Polite fight."

"Speak well of me when I'm gone, when I've been forgiven by the Assembly."

"My memory is good. You'll see. It'll rain when you come back. We won't forget that's what's going to happen. I'll watch for you night and day."

The promises flow from Ed's dear heart. Sad for us, the crew looks on, even Captain Randall. For a moment, I've never seen Ed this bewildered. Then he kisses me as though finally remembering the woman who, long ago, baked for him. Where did she go?

Lloyd is waiting. I'm sure Pastor Ron and he are praying for my salvation. I hear the Central Assembly of God singing "Hallelujah!

Hallelujah!" rejoicing as the saved have a right to do. *I can't leave the vessel. I can't go.* If I stay, the word of God will protect me. All of this comes beneath an orange moon the crew will watch when they gather later. I can't leave. There's no giving up on them. How could I comfort Marcus about his daughter, Orville about his wife? I've talked Bill through things. Ernie Schaub has requested my words to steady him. I trust these men. I'm their comfort; they are mine. Good has come from this seven years' voyage.

"Wait! The doll. I forgot it," Ed says. We call it the I Luv You doll. Last June Ed bought it. As Ed heads to my berth to retrieve the doll, I hope Orv, Ernie, Marcus, and the others change their minds and ask me to stay. By the fence, I just know a man whistles to himself and says, "Pss, pss, shh, sure." The whistle at the steam plant in Duluth goes off. Another starts far off on land when Ed comes back cradling I Luv You like he's accomplished something memorable.

Eventually, this mild night will turn toward winter. If I go, by midnight I'll be in Lloyd's arms, at least for an hour or a night. He's a cold, brittle sign-maker, a whistler under his breath. When winter comes, the city will be barren like him. Wind-blown Duluth. After hard snows, the city plows block our driveways as they clean the streets. The windrows, the snow ridges, will freeze there, freeze us in. Frost will build along the windowsills inside the houses. Ice will hang from the eaves outside. It'll be quiet and cold, but the ever-vigilant Lloyd Larson will keep me from turning up the thermostat to warm our house.

I can't abandon the crew, I say to myself.

It's like a test they've devised for me, though, a test of mercy for all. The forlorn Ed watches me even as I am being forgotten by him.

My departure being the will of God, I step tentatively with my doll onto the *Stimson's* gangway, only tentatively.

"We love you, Verna," they tell me until the whistle at the steam plant blows again.

"I love you, too, Verna," Lloyd says when we meet at the end of the dock. "Pss, pss, shh, sure."

THEY THAT GO DOWN TO THE SEA

Verna and Lloyd lived in a hillside bungalow from where they saw two cities, the surrounding countryside, and most wonderful, the great, deep lake sweeping its blue edge for miles along the shore. From the bungalow, the Larsons could also see ore docks, grain terminals, railroad yards, and the only oil refinery in the state of Wisconsin. They could see the interstate bridges connecting Duluth, Minnesota, and Superior, Wisconsin, plus the Aerial Lift Bridge over the harbor entry. The Aerial Bridge joins the downtown to a sandbar crowded with houses and traffic.

A month earlier, Mrs. Larson had returned from working on a Great Lakes freighter that hauled grain from the Twin Ports to Buffalo. By arrangement with herself (she'd stopped consulting her husband on anything), she'd been away 2,555 days. As the *Stimson's* second cook, she'd sailed the nine-month shipping season, taken vacations aboard, and worked as the vessel's shipkeeper during winter layup. Equating married life with shore life, she'd not left the boat in seven years.

Her husband wasn't fond of the relationship. His heart had been broken when he'd discovered her goodbye note taped to the bedroom mirror. He had no idea where she'd gone until a few days later he received a letter she'd sent to him when the mail boat came alongside the *Stimson* on the Detroit River. So bad had things grown in the Larson home over the years that Verna had had to leave. Her husband didn't yell, didn't throw things or threaten. Nothing like that. After fourteen years of marriage, he'd just grow quiet when things irritated him—say, the pepper shaker wasn't filled or the kitchen faucet dripped. His silence unnerved Verna, who at thirty-six back then was considerably younger than her Lloyd and relied too much on him for her well-being. "Lloyd, aren't you happy *again* today? What's wrong?" she'd finally asked before leaving. No answer from the silent Lloyd Larson.

Now ill with the heart failure that had begun after her departure, he was napping one morning before trying to catch a glimpse of his wife. Wanting to see her, he'd go to the pier on the waterfront when the *H.L. Stimson* was sailing in. He'd carry a sign he'd made with cardboard and a Magic Marker. Each time he brought a different sign. During the flurry of excitement that accompanies a vessel entering a port, he'd hold the cardboard sign high over his head. This day he'd brought a few signs, all with the same theme: I'm Dying of Heart Disease. I'm Dying of Lung Infections and Disorders. Help Me, God, Please Help Me!

Knowing there was no chance she'd leave the *Stimson* even after reading the startling news, he sat wearily in his car watching as the vessel tied up at one of the grain elevators in port. Sometime earlier, an ancient moon had risen. Across the bay and Minnesota Point, the harvest moon hung so low to earth that Lloyd thought he could ask the wise moon questions. "How far away are you from us tonight? Is God behind you out there somewhere? Will He spread His grace so my wife will believe my signs?" he asked.

Then she stood in front of the moon. Just like that, seven years had passed; and here she was, surprised at his appearance, how he'd done something with his hair, how he'd bought more fashionable glasses. "You look like my husband," she said.

Dumbstruck, Lloyd could say nothing, not even whistle, until he'd put her things in the trunk. When he finally spoke, his mouth was so dry the word "still" came out "shtill." "I am your husband.

We're shtill married." Then he clutched his chest. In the back were his hand-made signs. "I printed enough of them to get me through," he told Verna. "I didn't know if I'd live. It's good that you came home now. Praise God!"

When you're ill, you pace yourself. Though the doctors weren't certain Lloyd suffered heart problems, his chest hurt. Years earlier, a physician had written, "Patient presented at ER exhibiting symptoms." When Verna's husband was released from the cardiac unit that day long past, another doctor noted, wryly, on the medical chart, "Diagnosis: Heartbreak. Patient might be desolated by love." No doubt part of the mess at home was Verna's fault.

For Verna it was hard to sympathize, however, when, after two or three days, the house grew as quiet as it had been seven years before. (Yes, she was there. Can anyone be so heartless as to allow a husband to die alone and forgotten of lung ailments?) In the house she found more signs. Used and unused, they said things like, You Don't Know What You've Done To Me and I've Suffered So Much.

During these new days, the waiting period, Lloyd either rested on the couch or did his crossword puzzle or his Word Scramble in the daily paper. Then, remarkably, his failing health improved, though not a sound from him about this except when he whistled as he solved a difficult problem. Years earlier, his willful silence had caused her to leave. Now she wondered whether by returning she'd made the right decision. Word had reached her in the *Stimson's* galley via the handmade sign the crew told her about. She thought it was a joke, sending frightening news like this to her, but who jokes in such a way? She didn't know what to do.

"Tell me what you're stuck on in the crossword," she said now that she was with him again.

"An eight-letter word for a married man's lover. I have four letters, M-I-S-...-S."

But it was as though she didn't care to know the rest the more she realized—minute by minute—that she'd been duped. "Lloyd . . . Lloyd." Her comments and questions grew indistinguishable from the sounds in the house, the clock ticking, the furnace starting, the damper on the range hood clanking in a downdraft. The sounds became one. So, too, did the following make domestic life pleasing for Lloyd: the position of the furniture in the house, the smell of his morning coffee, the way Verna opened the drapes at a certain time of day, the way she scrubbed the sink and wiped the top of the stove. This is how life should be, thought Lloyd.

With such a picturesque view from their home, the Larsons owned a telescope. Through it, they marveled at the waves rolling to shore after a storm. They watched the morning traffic on the bridges. The variable-power spyglass had three draw tubes, one sliding into or out of another. When you matched the number 20× on one silver tube to the number 20× on another, sliding the focusing tube just slightly back and forth to adjust the view, the telescope magnified distant objects into a clean, sharp image of what a person wished to see. You could magnify to 15, 20, 25, or 30 power.

Depending on which side of a grain terminal the *H.L. Stimson* put in at, Verna might be able to magnify a deckhand when she peered through the telescope. Verna and the deckhand had kissed one night off of Copper Harbor. The deckhand and she had held each other and expressed true love off of Whitefish Point and Ashtabula. Once, as the *Stimson* made for safe harbor in Keweenaw Bay, they made love in a storm. Then Verna prayed and wondered about her future. Now she couldn't get their parting out of her mind. If Lloyd weren't dying, she'd never have left the *Stimson*. What about *my* heart, never mind yours, Lloyd! she thought to herself, the telescope helping her recall the man she loved and the crew she missed.

After Verna and the deckhand had kissed goodbye and a guilty Verna returned to her dying husband, her boat sailed for Buffalo. Now it was back. Through the spyglass, Verna saw the deckhand in the cold. On the bow, he shaded his eyes from the cold sun. Then he appeared to look for her.

"I'm through with the puzzle. Where are you?" Lloyd called to her up the stairs. When she didn't answer, he whistled as though he were on his way to solving a more difficult problem. The whistle was the only sound in the house that mattered. And there were plenty of sounds like the squeak of the dresser drawer, the clink of ice falling into the bucket in the freezer, or the way he folded the newspaper to concentrate on puzzles. Ah, for once marital harmony, felicity, Lloyd kept thinking. He began whistling something from *Cats*, his favorite, or from *Oklahoma!*

"It's quiet here. Let's get a parakeet," he said one morning when the wind stopped blowing.

Calculating the number of trips the *Stimson* would make yet this season to the Head of the Lakes, Verna didn't hear him—or what he said didn't register. She was thinking how quiet the house could be if she remained still and regulated her breathing. She was almost afraid to set the spyglass to its highest power for what it might do to her if she observed a deckhand blowing her kisses.

"Where are you? Are you upstairs? I can't climb the stairs in my condition," Lloyd called. He thought maybe something was bothering her. The amazed whistle came from downstairs, while upstairs, spyglass resting on the window ledge because of Verna's shaking hands and pounding heart, she fiddled with the eyepiece and whispered a deckhand's name.

Ed . . . Verna. Their relationship can be explained in the workings of the device she looked through and in the phrase "to telescope," which means "to slide or pass one within another like the cylindrical sections of a hand telescope." When she was done using the spyglass, she'd come downstairs where Lloyd said, "You've been hiding. Were you spying?" If she wasn't in the mood for this, she'd hold up the spyglass and ask whether he'd looked for *her* when the *Stimson* was in port. In that way the topic shifted to Lloyd and what he thought he'd been getting by marrying her years earlier.

Thinking of his heart, he'd stay on the couch until the *Stimson* sailed. Then his Verna would slide the eyepiece tube into the focusing tube, these into the largest tube, then all the draw tubes into the main part. "Where are you? You hide up there and look out. Please come down."

"Is your heart that bad?" she'd call down to him. "Can't you see another doctor?"

"You don't treat this trouble in a hospital. We have a leather case for the telescope. Why not put it away for the night?"

This was hard to do, for though the *Stimson* had departed, she could still look at the slip where the vessel had taken on grain. Sitting opposite him in the living room, coffee table between them, she wondered whether Lloyd was as ill as he claimed. Nine o'clock . . . 9:30 . . . 10 o'clock . . . 10:30. When he went to bed, she returned to the lookout. She couldn't open the telescope fast enough. At least she could keep in view the empty slip at the elevator. A few more nights weren't so lonely as a result of her vigil. My lord, how does a person endure the silence when she wants to be with someone, when she misses the crew she'd sailed with and comforted? What good was she to Lloyd? On the *H.L. Stimson*, men listened to her. On the *Stimson*, she'd fallen very much in love.

In the morning, Lloyd said up the stairs, "Are you there?" At noon, he asked, "Aren't you coming down?" At 5 p.m., he inquired, "Are you hungry? Tomorrow will you drive me to the hospital?"

"No," she said each time, though not so he heard. Or perhaps he did. Verna couldn't tell. How would she know he was down there, hand on the banister, while he calculated the effort it takes to climb fourteen carpeted stairs? In the darkness upstairs, he heard his wife's muttering and her fretful sighs.

When you're in love, a sigh and a beating heart can block out other things. Making it halfway up the stairs, Lloyd rested. His heart, you know. He sat there silently, telling himself that she was probably worn out from taking such good care of him. No doubt he'd find her at the desk planning what to prepare for his supper. He also thought his heart might burst when he got to the top step. Catching his breath outside the room, he whispered, "God help me if I go in."

When he peeked at her, Verna didn't hear him. Until the heartbeats in the room came louder and faster than her own and grew out of sync with them, all that mattered to her was at the grain terminal on the waterfront.

"What's out there?" Lloyd asked, startling her so that she dropped the spyglass.

"I didn't hear you."

"What's there?"

"Nothing. Leave me be."

"What are you looking for?" he asked.

"I don't know," she said, more out of frustration than out of an attempt to explain her feelings. "Why are you interested?"

"I'm tired of being downstairs."

"Do you remember I'd stay in the kitchen or living room for days with no word from you? That was when I lived here the first time. How long's it been since I returned? It appears your heart's improving."

"That's what you think. I don't see anything unusual," Lloyd told her as he stared through the window. "Trees are bare. Here's the hillside. There's Wisconsin. Where've you been, Verna? You should do something with your spare time."

"It's all spare time," Verna said, thinking how, on the *Stimson*, the opposite was true.

Then she did something to stop the questions. "Come here," she said encouraging him to look. Where her eye had rested, now Lloyd's took its place at the telescope. As he scanned the horizon, his fingers gripped the tubes.

"I can't focus. Your heart's here with me, Verna. I heard it. I heard you sighing. We're starting over. You heard my heart beat for you."

"We're out of focus," she said, her chest pounding. Poor, foolish Lloyd. The more he peered through the telescope lens, fiddling with the focusing tube as though that were the problem, the dimmer things grew. "You can't see a thing," she said, amazed at what he was doing.

"I've been sick," he said.

This time *she* focused the telescope. "I don't regret working on the boat," she said. "I don't regret the storms, the long winter layups. I don't regret my small berth. If you weren't dying, I'd have stayed aboard. I wrecked two precious lives for this, a lot more than two."

"Who are you talking about? Whose name are you hiding?"

"What name? I don't understand you. I don't call him anything. He's with me. We're together. You don't have to live in the dark. Make things clear. It's not one man I miss, it's the crew. I got something from them. They pleased my heart. Then you showed up with the announcement about your health."

"Who is he?" Lloyd persisted.

"A deckhand," Verna said.

Hearing her, Lloyd opened his eyes so wide that Verna feared what he'd do. For once, he was focusing totally on her. Then he whistled his famous whistle. It is a whistle that shows how deeply a person can be stunned, a whistle that attributes no guilt to the whistler but places the burden on the object or person that elicits the whistle. It is, the whistle, an amazed sound formed by tightening the upper lip, a whistle suggesting a person, the whistler again, has done nothing but has been aggrieved by his wife's taking of a lover. "Why, sure," he said as he shut the telescope. "I'll stay up here."

"The stairs are hard for you to walk down," she said, in some ways regretting what she'd told him, for now he'd be more righteous regarding his faithless, seafaring wife.

When she left in the morning, three people knew, or were soon to know, how things stood. Lloyd understood where she was headed, Verna knew she belonged on a grain boat bound for the Queen City of the Great Lakes, and the deckhand, the sailor whose mind was shot and who was soon to leave his job, exulted as much as he could at this turn of events. Through the power of magnification, the husband, wife, and lover had been able to magnify one another, sorting out what mattered to two of them.

When the deckhand spotted her on the dock, his heart leapt. He remembered her better than his crewmates thought he could. Such is the power of love. With the gray terminal towering above, the grain roaring out of the chutes into the holds, dust everywhere, he climbed down the gangway ladder. The *Stimson* to Verna was a mighty vessel that had brought her lover back, and everywhere grain dust mixed with the promise of the future. Verna and the deckhand kissed the way they'd kissed off of Copper Harbor.

Magnified by his wife's leaving, Lloyd Larson cried for a day and a half in the upstairs bedroom as he focused the telescope. When the sign-maker twice abandoned on the Duluth hillside got hungry, he ordered pizza. "Bring it right into the house and up to the room on the second floor," he said over the phone to the delivery boy. After that he had so little trouble magnifying his condition into something serious that he made it downstairs and to the hospital, where the doctors had no choice but to recommend surgery. When they'd taken sonograms, ghostly images of a beating heart, they found no normal heart but a bruised one. In the emergency room, he insisted, "This is all the fault of love."

Anyway, about the telescope, about all of this—the return home, the spying, the escape to the harbor, the sudden bursts of joy and pain in three hearts—all of it can be explained in few words: "to slide or pass one within another like the cylindrical sections of a hand telescope." Lloyd Larson, Verna Larson, and Edward Bronkowski, the deckhand on the *H.L. Stimson.*

Today, where is the telescope? On the windowsill in the room up the stairs Lloyd climbed to rescue his wife from the silence of love. The husband uses the telescope. He checks traffic on the bridges, scans the harbor, watches the moon rise. Once, he observed six or seven deer feeding on spilled grain in the railyards. Another time, he saw the Aerial Lift Bridge get stuck halfway up. Sometimes, he whispers to Verna. But when he does, he regrets it and thinks of his lovelorn heart. The clock ticks, the parakeet chirps, and he whispers, Lloyd does, until he gets tired of doing so. Then he goes downstairs.

"There, there, she'll be back," he says to Birdy, who, more than anyone or anything, loves the man and the sound of his voice. You almost wish the bird could respond, "There, there, sit and wait."

MOONGLADE

When my old man was alive, he'd read and reread his Polish newspapers. He'd speak no English on Sundays. In the evening, he'd drink a Polish beer. Brought from the old country, his pocket watch stands in its place of honor on the dining room table. Next to it, Ma has peonies in a vase. When I'm home from sailing, she heats up my favorite lunch. With a flour-sack bib around my neck, I make the Sign of the Cross, wind my dad's old-country watch, then dine on a chunk of Russian Rye and a can of stew. Done, I wipe my face and hands with a damp washcloth and signal for dessert.

How I got here after the accident starts with the wheelsman Orville Lee. He'll tell you how to sail from Buffalo to the Southeast Shoal on Lake Erie. "When you're heading upbound, lay a 248 course for sixty miles to pass off of Long Point, Ontario," he'll say. "Then steer the 249 course for 134 miles to one mile south of the shoal." He can tell you how to sail from the old lighthouse at Point Iroquois on Lake Superior to Outer Pancake Shoal, and from there, home. By talking to him and studying lake charts, I've learned that vessels contact Seaway Long Point, VHF-FM channel 11, to report to the Coast Guard when off of Long Point. I've learned that oil- and gas-drilling towers in Canadian waters warn you with a flash of light and a two-second blast from a fog signal beacon followed by eighteen seconds of silence. This information comes from me, Ed Bronkowski, a sailor on the *H.L. Stimson*. I also got some of it from Orville Lee and the Army Corps of Engineers' Lake Superior Chart No. 9.

Last week, with the vessel following the 302 course a little beyond Southeast Shoal, my brain began shutting down. In the night, with the *Stimson* bound for Pelee Point Light, I'm getting a drink of water when she rolls in a stiff northwest wind. Depending on the height of the waves, the strength of the wind, and how much cargo or ballast we're carrying, a vessel can roll ten or fifteen degrees around that shoal. When she did, I fell. I hit my head. The water glass broke. When Bull LaVoy, the mate, found me in my berth, I was sitting in my underpants, knee cut, face bloody. I told him, "Lemme go on with the fight, Bull. I got my jab working."

"Fight's over, kid," he said when they put me on the mail boat in the Detroit River to bring me to the hospital. For a few days, I could recall the incident, then I'd forget what happened. I figured the cut to my noggin and the general condition of my brain after losing twenty pro fights had done me in. With my seniority as a deckhand, fifteen years of lugging mooring cables along docks, scraping paint, sweeping spilled cargo overboard, and hosing down decks, I'd earned the right to a week off from the *Stimson*, I thought. When I called the head office, the secretary said, "Captain Randall phoned in the accident report. How do you feel, Mr. Bronkowski?"

"I got a concussion and had a seizure from what's on my mind. I'm taking time off. I've got frequent flyer miles to go home on. In Superior, I'll get in fighting shape."

"Let us know when you're better, and I'll tell you what port to meet your boat in. You're pretty old for boxing. My husband saw you fight in Youngstown."

"The Joe Lovely bout. Did I win?" I ask, hoping to save her the embarrassment of talking to a loser.

"That's right. That was the name. I wouldn't advise boxing anymore," she said.

"Did I beat Joe Lovely?" I kept asking after the line went dead.

Now the accident, the Detroit River, and the hospital are behind me. I recover fast. The mail has brought get-well cards from Verna Larson, my girlfriend on the *H.L. Stimson*, and from Bull LaVoy. Safe at Ma's, I wonder if I'll remember anything again. I know Merrihew Lakes Transit is a good shipping company. I know I have a cousin, Leon Adjukiewicz, in Milwaukee and two brothers here in Superior, the older one Al and the younger one Walt. I have Walt's kids, too, my nephews Keith and Andy. I've been to every Great Lakes' port and fought in half of them. I've sailed on straightdeckers and self-unloaders hauling grain, salt, ore, and cement. I remember this, yet one of Walt's kids says to me yesterday, "What's the distance from the sun to the earth? How old's America's oldest city? Name one kind of dragonfly."

Things like that puzzle me. Why not ask about the coal pile at the power plant in Ashland or the *Stimson*'s turbine engines? I wanted to swear at the kid, but not in front of his little brother who's eight or nine years old. In honor of our heritage, I call the younger one Andrzej. It's pronounced "Awn-jay." He worships me. He visits me at Ma's. When I'm asleep on the couch because it's stuffy upstairs, she will wake me, no matter the hour, and say, "Andy's here."

Coming to, I remember who I lost fights to in the Omaha Civic Center and the Milwaukee Auditorium. I remember how my old man would call me "*Bokser*" in Polish and shake his head in disappointment. To remain this sharp, I must be younger than fifty-one. I can never remember.

"Is Butch, my manager, alive? How old am I?" I ask Ma.

"Old enough," she says.

She worries about me when I fly off the handle at the TV or newspaper articles. I wonder how long she will put up with it. Still, Ma, my nephew, and Verna Larson on the boat care about me. That's why Ma's up early trying to please me with what she cooks and bakes and why Andrzej has come over today.

"Uncle Ed, will you help me?" he asks. Very gently he touches my stitches as if by tickling them he can get me to agree.

"Help how? I'm getting off of watch. I can't go anywhere at 6 a.m.," I tell him, pretending to be on the *Stimson*. Banged up like I am, the living room couch will do me fine for now, I think. Then I say to myself and Andrzej things that Pa used to mutter: "Próżnowanie początkiem wsztstkiego żłego . . . Idleness is the root of all evil" or "Kto rano wstaje, temu Pan Bóg daje . . . Who rises early, to him God gives." He likes hearing the Polish, but this don't stop him from making his request.

"My brother has to help Mr. DuBose look for dragonflies. He's with the DNR," he says.

Even when I wash up, the kid's talking. As I complain to my beat-up face in the bathroom mirror, I picture him and Ma in the kitchen—the kid with the curious look and round, sweet face and the gray-haired lady in a housecoat trying to catch her breath because of breathing problems. I picture my old man beside me in the mirror shaking his head saying "*Bokser, bokser.*"

When I come in freshly shaved, Andrzej's bragging about me. How can I not love him? He's a big fan. "Uncle Ed said that" or "Uncle Ed did this," he tells Ma as she ties the flour sack about me and hands me a napkin.

"*Bigos* for lunch later?" Ma asks when Andrzej stops for a second.

"Bigos," I say. "My girlfriend don't serve it on the boat."

"What kind of bread with it? I have to go to the store."

"Pumpernickel," I say, finishing my coffee and cinnamon toast. "We should be home by noon."

Once Ma wipes my chin, we leave for the morning. Keith, the youthful scientist, needs my supervision. At his house, my brother's car stands outside. He's a Union Pacific switchman in the Allouez railyard.

"What's your old man doing?" I ask the kid.

He stares at his iPhone. "He's upstairs."

"I'm getting ready for work," Walt calls down. "Take both sets of keys to your ma's car, Keith." My sister-in-law, who's gone already, rides to work with a neighbor. If I don't go to the bog today to supervise Keith, it'll mean no fun for the nine-year-old nephew while his uncle's home.

I'd rather play with Andrzej's remote-control cars or the Lego kit than go out there. Knowing my head's been punched over the years, the doctors advise me, "Try to put bad thoughts from your mind." Verna tells me this, too—thoughts like how the older nephew, Keith, never thanks me for birthday cards and money or how he gets sullen when I talk.

"Tell him a Blue Darner is one name of a dragonfly, Uncle Ed. Another is Twelve-Spotted Skimmer. Keith has a book full of their pictures," Andrzej says. He's smart for his age. Running to the car, he climbs in back while the other nephew is still texting.

"Because of my head injuries, I don't remember if dragonflies are smaller than birds," I tell them.

"*Come on!*" Keith says, not believing I wouldn't know this. "I bet you saw them on the Cuyahoga River when it was burning in 1969. Mr. DuBose told me about the river fire. He's getting me a job someday."

"That was in Cleveland. I was too young to leave home then. Don't worry, I've seen things you wouldn't imagine."

"Like what?"

"Like how we were sailing off of Copper Harbor when a flock of birds landed on the *Stimson*. They were migrating. The captain called them warblers. They settled down with us and slept. We were heading southeast to Whitefish Point, they were heading north, so they lost time."

Thinking about this quiets the scientist. Sitting in front, I watch him drive. He has blond hair a shade darker than Andrzej's. Never subjected to the boxing ring or to life, Keith's face and heart are scar-free. Something gives him a defiant look. When he admires himself in the rearview mirror, I think it's impolite to do so, especially with others around. He's not as handsome as he thinks. His nose ain't perfect. Maybe right now his life ain't perfect. Maybe he needs a swat.

"Do you want to see how *you* look, Uncle Ed?" he asks.

"Won't be necessary," I say, needing no reminder of my curled-up ears and swollen cheekbones.

Why do I think Keith laughs at me? I fit out the *Stimson* for the shipping season, make a few trips up and down the lakes, return home with head busted open, and right away I'm angry when I see him. Dear Jesus, keep me from going crazy. This is what I'm peeved at. If he catches me in mistakes, he says, "No, it isn't like that" or "You're wrong about that." Andrzej, the younger one, knows I ain't bright. I pray *he'll* love his Uncle Ed and remember me and talk about my accomplishments in the ring someday.

On the map open on my knees, I trace my finger along the county road. "It looks like a sharp turn," I tell Keith when we enter the woods that go for miles and miles. In my other hand, I hold the dragonfly book Andrzej's passed to me from in back. "Slow up," I tell his brother. "I'm a wheelsman."

"How do you figure that, Uncle Ed? You said you were a deck-hand," Andrzej says.

"Get your stories straight," Keith says.

"I've seen breakwaters, that's all I know," I say, which follows nothing the boys have been talking about. If I make no sense sitting with a blank look on my face, Keith will know I'm hopeless. "In Huron, Ohio, one breakwater only hooks partway to shore. This causes sand to build up," I tell him. "You must go far left of the right breakwater so as not to run aground."

"Who cares about Huron?" Keith asks. Angry I came today, he expects some point in what I'm telling them. Driving too fast, he almost steers us off the road. Maybe he should slow down. He should understand I've fought in Indiana and Nebraska. I have jumped from the fantail of the *H.L. Stimson* to rescue a sailor in the St. Mary's River. Keith should learn from me, but he sends messages and listens to his hip-hop singers through the earbuds of that thing.

"I told you ease off the gas pedal."

"What was the point of your story?"

"What story?"

"The Huron one."

"What about it?" I ask, but it's no use trying to remember.

Instead, I recall that our trip to the bog has brought us past the creosote plant, Four Corners, Amnicon Lake. I can recall that twenty-six thousand people live in Superior. It's the biggest city in Douglas County. When you think you're in wild country outside of town, up the road it's always wilder, the forest deeper. I sense this mystery when we're east of the turn. My mind is clear on this, too: The smirk on the older kid's face.

Keith's dragonfly book says that when American Emerald dragonflies breed they "prefer bog ponds and boggy lakes, forest ponds, fens and sedge marshes." In the air, the males "hover and dart, hover and dart." In the book's beautiful photos, they have bright green eyes, a yellow ring on their abdomen, and two sets of wings with a triangle mark on the front wings.

"What's a fens?" I ask to calm my anger at Keith. "Why don't you call the fellow you're writing to?"

"Who calls? We text," he says. "We don't read books either. I can find dragonfly pictures online." Slowing the car, he asks the little sprout whether he's going wading with him now that we're here.

Where we leave the paved road and go onto the dirt one, it's like the earth floats on bogs. What's the word for this place, prime-something . . . primeval? The bog pond, 150 feet across, ends at a wall of trees. Covered by lily pads and duckweed the way the pond is, I will not blame Andrzej for staying out of it. One thousand years will pass, yet all will remain the same, the tall grass, the forest, the screech of birds. In among this is the DNR man. Waving my hands to keep away blackflies, I start talking to him when Keith interrupts me. "I only have a driver learner's permit, Mr. DuBose. My uncle had to come today."

Mr. DuBose is thirty years younger than me. He wears a bush hat. "Did the boy tell you I have extra waders in the truck?"

"I'm not in shape to exert myself."

"It's too deep to walk in," Andrzej says.

"You don't need waders. Roll up your jeans, Andy. The peat holds you up. The dragonfly skeletons we get are ex-u-vi-ae." Keith pronounces the syllables slow as though otherwise I won't understand.

My shirt is soaked from the humidity. When Keith tells me not to stir up flies in this place, my head feels worse. No rule says a man must accept insults. I should surprise him with a jab to the chin. "You heard of me, Mr. DuBose?"

"You were the boxer."

"My brother was in the Marines."

"Tough family," Mr. DuBose says. "The field work I do is safer than boxing. By the way, Ebony Boghaunters emerge in late May. They're a 'glacial relict,' a holdover from thousands of years ago. We flag spots where we find their exoskeletons. That way we create a map of the bog and the exoskeletons using the flags' coordinates. The Kennedy's Emerald emerged three days ago, June fourth. We collected six exoskeletons."

"A relict is like you, Uncle Ed, a remnant of an otherwise extinct organism," Keith says.

I don't catch his meaning at first, then things fall silent. It isn't right for the son of a bitch to say this about me.

In the heat and stillness, Andrzej knows I'm angry. "Your brother don't take me serious. He don't like me. Do I look stupid in the bib at Ma's? I ask, watching the scientists wade through the water to the shady side of the pond.

"That's not it," Andrzej says.

"He don't know what a seiche is, I bet. It's pretty scientific. See, Andrzej, I learn stuff. You can't be blamed for not knowing the term. You're young. I know you'll be a sailor. I can see you're captain material."

"Do you have a girlfriend?" he asks, catching me off guard. "Keith's girlfriend usually drives him here in her ma's car. He's a year behind her in high school. She has her license. Her name's Doreann. She wants to be a scientist. That's who he's texting. She was tired this morning and didn't want to take him. 'Get Barnacle Bill,' Keith told me when he needed a ride. 'He has time to take us.' Some days Keith is sad about her. They always argue over things."

"I have a girlfriend. She bakes pastries and pies on the boat. I got a card from her. I gave her a doll once that says I Luv You on it."

Trying to remember if there's more Andrzej's asked me, I tell him about another girlfriend. "When I was fifteen, I'd go to her house. I found her a stone shaped like a heart. Years later, I got married but not to Mae. When my career's going great, Mae shows up one night for an Ed 'the Bronko' Bronkowski fight. I'm coming out of the ring, everybody congratulating me, and I see her in the doorway. She's a nurse. It's 1988. When my trainer wipes my face, I give my old girlfriend a hug. 'I saved the heart-shaped stone you gave me, Eddie,' she says. She could've forgotten me."

When I look over, Andrzej's flushed with heat. Maybe he's preoccupied with his brother. The frail Andrzej Bronkowski won't be a seaman. Surrounded by the drowsy buzz of the pond, he can hardly keep his eyes open. The poor kid, why should he care if someone saved me a stone? He's got important things on his mind. With a stalk of tall grass, I shoo flies and mosquitoes from him.

"Will you show me a dragonfly, Uncle Ed?" he asks.

"Remember how we played Legos?"

"We can play laser tag later," he says. "I think Keith's sad."

Then he gets too tired to care about anything. His head lolls against a tree. I realize again how everything's in place: the thick, silent woods, the quiet flutter of birds, Mr. DuBose's soft voice, the ride here, my fight career. On the bog, things follow a natural order, and I know I've done kind deeds for others like Ma and Verna on the *Stimson*, and Mae did kind things for me as did Bull LaVoy when he found me injured.

The book says dragonflies hover, zigzag, and fly about. They disappear, return, disappear like my wife after our marriage. Across from us, Keith and Mr. DuBose place their flags.

To see if Andrzej's awake, I say, "Pretend we're on the breakwater at our end of Lake Superior. Your Uncle Ed's a boy. I've ridden my bike to the end of Wisconsin Point fourteen miles one-way from home to see if what I heard is true about the lake. Are you still listening, Andrzej? In the distance, I see Duluth. Where I am, the channel enters Superior Bay. No one's around. It's quiet. The concrete breakwater that forms one side of the channel extends 150 feet into the lake. You can walk to the end. In the water halfway out are boulders that driftwood gets trapped on. The boulders stabilize the breakwater and the shore. You ever gone there?"

"With my dad," Andrzej says, though he's sleepy.

"In the story I'm telling, all day the lake's been quiet. Now the water laps up and down against the breakwater. There's no breeze. When the day's been still, how could the water on Lake Superior start moving like this? It's mysterious. Except for the lake, all I see are the woods of Wisconsin Point and the shore curving to the other lighthouse."

I hope wherever Andrzej is in dreams, he'll hear this and remember. "On the eastern shore of Lake Superior, the water's piled up from the storm that pushed it there," I tell him. "The water has to return. It's called a 'seiche' when this happens—like if you tilt a bowl of water, when you put down the bowl the water returns from one side to even out the surface. I read about this in a book. The great blue summer spread before me that day on the breakwater. I was fifteen. Then the lapping water. I saw it when it started. I was a boy like you and your brother."

Saying "seiche" or "moonglade" or "scintillation," which is the reason stars appear to move in the night sky, I'm teaching the one young person in the world who cares about me. Talking to a sleeping Andrzej reminds me of the hopes I had when I liked Mae Shaul or when I loved my wife. All I asked was for things to work out. Now I have words to remember when everything's gone. I've held on to them. I've never told Andrzej or anyone: Seiche. Scintillation. Moonglade.

Keith's book describes the habitat of dragonflies, what they eat, how, once they've left their larval shell and are in the "teneral stage," sometimes it takes an hour for their wings to dry before they fly away. A group of dragonflies is a "dazzle." Leaving my nephew, I examine one by the pond. As delicately as I've held my wife's hand in marriage or my newborn son at baptism, I place my index finger beside the Ebony Boghaunter. The finger was broke in a fight. I nudge the Boghaunter close with the tip of another finger broke in a fight. Wings moving, it feels lighter than moonlight. Like Uncle Ed Bronkowski, it is a relict.

When I say "seiche, scintillation, moonglade," I think the words have never been spoken together before. Nudging the Ebony Boghaunter into my palm, I repeat the words, knowing the dragonfly's ancestors hovered about when I was born, when I was in school, when I fought out of Butch Maeder's gym, then when Adele, my wife, left with my son and I didn't know where they went. During this moment when I feel the creature's weight and see its delicate, transparent wings outlined in black, it's as if I recall every opportunity for beauty I've seen and lost. I whisper, "I have to love one final thing. Something has to remember I loved it," so that when Andrzej sees the Ebony Boghaunter, he might not forget it. Memories will tie us together the way beauty ties everything.

As my nephew stirs, the Boghaunter rises. "Wait! Let me show you to Andrzej," I say, still feeling the spot where the dragonfly's rested. "Look! Look!" I call to my nephew as though I've found something for Mae Shaul thirty-five years ago. I point to the pond where small wings glitter. For a second, Andrzej doesn't know what I'm pointing to. Then I think he spots it. "I believe you," he calls.

"I held it in my hand. It stayed with me, Andrzej. You should've seen it."

He looks like he's confused about where he is. When he rubs his eyes to wake up, it's like only at that moment he remembers his brother walking in the pond and Uncle Ed home from the lakes. I have faith that Andrzej has seen what I have if only in his dreams, that he'll remember me when I'm in a rest home, which is where they put you when you have no words. I hope someday he will bring me a book with pictures and say that he has held an Ebony Boghaunter and whispered to it.

When we walk over to Keith and Mr. Dubose, my hand on Andrzej's shoulder for support, he says, "Tell me what is moonglade? I was falling asleep when you started to tell me. I want to remember."

"It's the pattern bright moonlight makes on a large expanse of water," I tell him. "Say you're upbound for Superior on the *H.L. Stimson* from some port on the lower lakes. Say you're getting off of watch and ahead of you the moon is bright and hundreds of warblers surround you. Moonglade is so bright it lights your way."

"What are the other words?"

"Seiche. Do you remember seiche? Do you remember what scintillation is, when stars appear to move because of changes in the atmosphere?"

"Yes, I do," he says as I try explaining further.

"I memorized the meaning. Scintillation means 'rapid changes in the brightness of a celestial body.'"

"Like it's God's shadow falling across the sky?"

"That's its cause," I tell him.

When I'm done with the words I'm thankful to remember, I don't feel as bad about how life has turned out. But I'm very sad for the older kid. I thought he had everything going for him with his straight As, a girlfriend, a driver learner's permit, and Mr. Dubose of the DNR. Now that I've heard about Keith, I'm not angry. He has his own sorrow with her. He's heartbroken by love when I glance across at him. I wouldn't want to go through such heartbreak again. I won't have to worry about things like this much longer.

What the younger boy and I share about beauty now is as important as what Keith is experiencing about love. I have held a dragonfly and Andrzej is remaining a child long enough for me to join him once I forget the things that my memory won't hold onto.

"Don't grow up. Please don't," I say to him the way I said "Wait! Wait!" to the Ebony Boghaunter. Maybe in a few months or a year, I'll need Andrzej to tie my bib at the table, need him to tell me stories of the sea.

In these last days with him, I'll remember a morning when dragonflies, a dazzle of them, emerge and sparkle above the pond. I've never seen anything like it. They stop and hover. They dart and zigzag. You can hear their wings beating the air. It is a kind of magic song or prayer I cannot decipher.

THE SHIPMASTER'S BALL

Ed was used to being lowered to the pier. When they swung me over in the bosun's chair, I hung on for dear life. After the *Stimson* locked through the Soo and continued down the St. Mary's River for the lower lakes, we took a room at the Seaway Inn near a Burger King on Ashmun Street. There we were, the woman who'd left her husband and the man who missed his wife after many years. That didn't stop us from falling in love.

In the room, I drew the curtains, unplugged the clock. Our rule was never to ask the time. And so we lay there, happy when we touched. The *Stimson* would cross Lake St. Clair with a load of grain from the Dakotas, pass Grassy Point at the western edge of Lake Erie, pass Lorain, Cleveland, Ashtabula before arriving at the General Mills elevator in Buffalo. We'd board her on the return trip. Until then, we'd hold each other during the off-season for tourists.

When evening came, Ed got our supper. Done eating, he put the Styrofoam containers outside the room, then checked the do not disturb sign and locked the door. In bed, we whispered about what our lives meant. We'd made mistakes, helped others, even loved, though for me never deeply except during the first years of marriage to Lloyd Larson of Duluth, Minnesota. Now I loved Eddie Bronkowski.

I have no idea what time it was when we heard someone in the hallway going, "Shh—"

"Shh—" I said to Ed. I told him how Lloyd would say "Shh—" whenever I said anything. When I ended up with no voice in our house, I'd *had* to leave, which is when I'd made my way to the *Stimson* taking on grain at Harvest States Elevator in Superior.

Ed knew this about me, but like other things, he'd forgotten. I never blamed him for forgetting. A prizefighter who'd lost three quarters of his pro bouts, Ed was the grand champion of my heart. "Shh—" we heard the man again as a door closed down the hall, a lock clicked, a chain secured a room.

"Could that be him?" Ed asked.

Later, we heard someone whistle as though wishing to send a message. On the second floor of the Seaway, three or four of us might have been the only guests.

Knowing the door was secure and that Lloyd, my husband, couldn't have possibly found me in Sault Ste. Marie, I said, "Tell me a sweet story." But the desk clerk fumbling outside the door with the Styrofoam containers from our supper distracted us. Instead of listening to a love story, I studied a map of the Upper Peninsula and paged through tourist brochures. Ed wondered whether to keep the motel stationery.

We watched an old movie on TV, a swashbuckler, then fell asleep. At daybreak, Eddie told me about the Shipmaster's Ball. "The captains of the *Arthur M. Anderson*, the *Beagley*, the *Walter J. McCarthy*, and other boats came to it. They wore dark blue dress uniforms with gold buttons. Gold stripes circled their jacket cuffs. The company's names—Cleveland Cliffs, Interlake Steamship, Ford Motor Company, Canada Steamship—were embroidered on the blue uniforms. It was something all right, the band, the champagne. I remember the women in beautiful dresses and sparkling jewelry. The port director, the mayors of Duluth, Superior, Two Harbors, and Thunder Bay, harbor pilots, tug owners, everyone was dressed up to celebrate the coming of the shipping season."

"It was beautiful, wasn't it?" I asked.

"I opened car doors, hung up coats, gave people directions. Every time somebody left the ballroom, I watched the band. The dancers swirled around."

A day and night passed with stories about the Shipmaster's Ball, about Lake Michigan seen through sea smoke on a January morning, about the ice caves of the Apostle Islands. Then afternoon became evening on a day in the shipping season. When Ed went to get a meal for us, I packed our things. We had a few hours before the *Stimson* returned through the Soo.

I'll tell you what love is: It is everything. For years, the crew of the *Stimson* had looked out for me, respected me just as I'd cared for them. Then Ed came into my life. "Ed, I love you for telling me about the ball and for everything else," I whispered. With him out, I packed our clothes, our toiletries, the stationery. I knew the next time we were apart might be the last for us. During those November days in the Seaway, we'd talked of seafarers. I'd dreamt that the captain of the *Stewart J. Cort* had invited me to dance. After Ed returned from Burger King and we had BK Broilers, fries, and pieces of apple pie in little boxes, I danced with him. We held each other.

"Someday, I won't remember you," he said when it was time to leave.

"We'll put our memories in these envelopes," I said. "One for you, one for me. If we get lost, people can direct us back to the Seaway Inn, Sault Ste. Marie."

"Do we seal the envelopes?"

"I'm not sure," I said.

What he did next surprised me. He'd hidden the two crowns in a Burger King bag. "These are beautiful," I told him when he placed one of the crowns on my head. He arranged it perfectly. "Will you put a crown on me?" he said, then held my face in his hands.

For once in our lives, we were important. A deckhand and a second cook. As we walked down Ashmun Street to the locks in Sault Ste. Marie, we were the works wearing our crowns with rubies in them. Ed said if he was working the Shipmaster's Ball this night, he'd let us in with our crowns on, which would identify us as VIPs.

Soo Control decides which vessel uses which lock. The Poe Lock is 1,200 feet long, 110 feet wide, 32 feet deep. The MacArthur Lock is shorter. It takes 40 to 60 minutes to pass through them. Vessels rise 21 feet if they're upbound. We were upbound. Once a vessel has locked through the Soo, it's free to proceed into the deepest and coldest lake. I can tell you that love, real love, is everything in life, and the last thing you want to do is forget it.

Dear Ed,

I took a cab to see you. The crew says hi! I guess I missed your nephews and your brother. I hear they visit. That's a relief that they'll drive out from Superior. Many relatives wouldn't do that with you not knowing them when they arrive.

"You can put that manila envelope on the dresser," the nurse tells me. "I'll see that Ed's brother Alphonse gets it."

The letter I'm now writing will go inside the 9 × 12 manila envelope I've brought from the *Stimson*. There's already one sealed envelope inside of the manila envelope. The sealed one is on stationery from a motel in the Soo.

I should say that Captain Randall is his usual self, Ed. He likes his ice cream, this month Rocky Road. Ernie Schaub had to leave the Stimson in Buffalo. He's had pneumonia. He's cured now, though. Last winter, Bill Lamson completed some of the house projects he'd been talking about. Remember him? We're all fine.

Just as I started writing this letter, the nurse asked if I wanted coffee. "No," I said.

I do want things, though. I want you better. It's hard seeing you like this. My heart breaks.

This morning in the galley, I tried beginning a letter. I figured for once Orv Lee could make his own Purina. Then I started putzing around anyway. Now in your room at Middle River Health Care outside of Superior, Wisconsin, I'm writing this. I touch your face while you rest. "Remember me? Remember the Henry L. Stimson?" I whisper. "You once told me about your brother Al. He was in the military. I'm happy he visits. Please come back to me, Ed. Please remember our memories."

There's nothing and everything in the manila envelope I'm leaving here. I'll put this handwritten letter inside of it. When he finds the envelope that says "The Seaway Inn / 900 Ashmun Street / Ste. Sault Marie, Michigan" on it, Ed's brother, your brother, Ed, will hold it and say to someone, to your nephews, "There's nothing in it. Feel how empty the envelope is." *But you and I know better. It's my envelope from the Soo. It was near the end when we stayed in the Seaway Inn. We'd sealed two envelopes that night—yours, mine—and said our memories would remain inside them forever. You were going away in your mind. I was staying behind. We promised to keep loving. Now what else do we have but memories sealed in paper envelopes, sealed by glue?*

This is what the letter will instruct your brother, Alphonse, to do: On this floor for dementia patients, give the Seaway Inn envelope to Ed, my beloved. Tell him to notice my perfume on it. Tell him to notice my kiss and my tears. Help him to open the Seaway Inn envelope. Do it very, very gently until our beautiful memories, Ed's and mine, join forever.

THIS IS YOUR LIFE

When Ralph Edwards introduces celebrities on his TV show, he says "Dinah Shore" or "Dick Van Dyke, *this is your life!*" After the applause, he goes on in dramatic fashion, "You were born in the small town of Oswego, New York," or maybe it's Klamath Falls, Oregon, or Des Moines, Iowa. Next, Mr. Edwards offers the celebrity clues about the people from his or her past waiting backstage. "Who called you 'Dumplin' when you were five years old?" he asks. "Who bought you your first bike when you were nine?" In high school when I watched the show with my ma, she'd say, "Here we go, Al." When Dinah Shore walked out, Ma's tears would fall. I wanted to cry, too, but I was joining the Marines.

"Nineteen-year-old Alphonse Bronkowski," Mr. Edwards is saying now, "a little over a month ago on your last afternoon in Infantry Training Regiment, Camp Pendleton, California, the training instructor made you do fifty push-ups in the Santa Ana winds before letting you board the bus to L.A. for a plane trip home on leave. Your Western Airlines flight stopped in Phoenix, Albuquerque, and Denver before landing in Minneapolis. From there, you took the Greyhound to Superior. Back in California now, you've been assigned to Staging Battalion, Camp Pendleton, where you're preparing to go overseas to Okinawa. This is *your* life, Alphonse Bronkowski."

This is my life, Mr. Ralph Edwards, mid-November.

On weekend liberty, I'm waiting for Private Roy Elkins in a downtown Los Angeles movie house. I watch *Ten Days in a Nudist Camp* and keep my eyes on the moviegoers looking for someone to join them. There must be thirty men in here. Sitting alone in the back, dreaming that I'm in a nudist camp, I remove my jacket.

On screen, six or seven sun-worshippers toss beach balls as a man's voice explains the joy of naked living. "See how outdoor frolic suits these beauties?" he asks. Thank heavens, it was warm in the theater when Private Elkins and I first came in three hours ago. I'm alone now, no Elkins. He's taken off. I want to join the nudists on the volleyball court. But they're on a movie screen, and I'm watching them. Making my shirt into a pillow, I rest a little.

"Alphonse Bronkowski, you were born in a small Wisconsin town," Mr. Edwards says. "Your mother takes care of the house. Your dad labors at the flour mill. You have a baby brother. Instead of marrying your girlfriend, you enlisted in the Marine Corps. That was six months ago. This and that have happened since then. Your main regret is you're lonely. Who'll be the first to greet you on *This Is Your Life*? Your parents, Frank and Evelyn Bronkowski, carrying your baby brother Ed? Your girlfriend, Willa Beecher, who's traveled with them from Wisconsin? Your drill instructors from the recruit depot?"

Mr. Edwards, Mr. Ralph Edwards, I'd like to tell *you* something. Later you can tell me about my life. Last week, Lance Corporal Freddie Wilson charged the guys in Staging Battalion two bucks to attend his party at a motel. We listened to Junior Walker records and drank until his girl told us to go and I stumbled into an Oceanside tattoo parlor. Drawings hung from the walls. The one with the downward-pointing dagger read "Death before Dishonor." Another had a Marine Corps bulldog with a World War One helmet, strap around his chin, and a spiked leather collar.

The tattoo artist chain-smoked. A sandwich with wilted lettuce lay beside the ink and needles.

"Spell out her name," he'd said, putting out his cigarette. "Keep your arm still."

"No, don't write her name. Just draw a cross," I said to him before I passed out. I was dreaming of Willa when I got tattooed. "We're done," the man said, dabbing my arm with cotton. "If it gives you trouble, come back in."

"What?"

"The Willa tattoo," he said.

I wondered how much I'd told him when I was there. Why didn't she write me if this was *my* life, I thought, before remembering how, when I was home, she told me we couldn't go out anymore.

Now in a movie house in Los Angeles, I'm half-naked. When Private Elkins and I came in, it was dark outside. We'd walked around downtown, eaten a hamburger, got whistled at by men in Pershing Square, peeked in a place where the sign read "Ten Cents A Dance" like we were in a 1930s movie. Where was Elkins? Two hours ago, bored with the movies, I told him I was taking off.

"Do what you want, Al," he said. "I'm not going back to Camp Pendleton before I have to. It's only eleven o'clock at night," he'd said, reminding me it was one of our last Saturdays stateside.

I froze outside. When I returned in an hour, this time Elkins was Missing in Action. Maybe he was looking for me at the bus station.

At one o'clock, *Ten Days in a Nudist Camp* starts anew. This, *Naked Venus*, and *Blonde and Beautiful* will run tonight, tomorrow, next week—an eternity of nudie movies. In this one, the narrator says, "Sun-worshippers love fresh air. Here they come. See them wave. Let's watch Gretchen. It's time for her swim."

I like Gretchen. If I was in the movie, I'd be known as Naked Adonis.

Mr. Ralph Edwards, famous TV host, last week in the barracks I asked Private Elkins, "What's my tattoo look like? Before I left home, Ma told me 'Don't ruin the body the Lord's given you.'"

"There's a cross on it and your girlfriend's name. The colored parts of the tattoo are swollen. Otherwise, it's pretty neat. I guess your body's not so precious. By the way, I picked up your mail. You got a letter from your old man."

"Read it to me. I'm hungover. Does he mention Willa?"

When he's done, I say, "Nothing about her again? Why wouldn't she write to me?"

"You got me. The next time I have a chance I'm going to L.A. to look for Steve McQueen, my favorite actor. He lives up there."

"So does Chuck Connors, the Rifleman," I tell him.

If I was on the Ralph Edwards show, who would Mr. Edwards bring out? I wonder again and again. My grade school nun? Ma's entire rosary sodality? When I called Willa long distance last week, no one answered. By now, I think Elkins has started back to Camp Pendleton. It's ninety-five miles down the Pacific Coast Highway.

I'll watch the movies, then sleep. Gretchen is as blonde as my girlfriend. Retrieving a beach ball, she tosses it toward the pool. If I imagine hard and squint my eyes, Gretchen becomes Willa who's not written me since I came back to California. Willa is Gretchen.

Hearing a commotion, I reach for my shirt. A moviegoer adjusts his eyes to the dark. I am thinking of how it'd be living with Willa when the man sits nearby. With all the empty places in a theater that once must have been beautiful, why does the newcomer choose this row? After a sigh, the other men return to what they were doing. When I turn around, he asks me, "Are you Herbert?"

"No," I say. I'm startled when his fingertip traces the outline of the cross on my arm. "This has to do with Herbert," he says. "We were to meet. I'm Joey from La Mirada. It's a suburb. I teach high school there. What brings you in?"

"The movies," I tell him.

"Are you a nudist?"

"It sure sounds like a healthy life."

Wondering if I'm dreaming, I pinch myself. In boot camp, was I the guidon carrier? Was Huber the biggest screwup ever in Platoon 146? When this man, Joey, asks if he can hold my jacket when I get my cigarettes, I say, "Maybe." When he asks, do I have a cigarette for him, I say, "Only a Lucky Strike." When he asks, do I enjoy sitting like this, I say, "I want to be a nudist."

"You've still got clothes on. What kind of nudist is that?" he asks.

"I'm learning about naturism. I'm glad it's dark in here. Are you going to be a nudist?" Then I think of home, how when I return stateside, half of my three-year hitch will be over.

At 1:30 a.m, *this* is my life. As I think of Ma saying, "Don't defile your body, which is made in the image and likeness of God," the man touches my arm again. "Do you love Herbert? Are you sure? Will you help me look for him?" When he motions to me, I gather my things.

Paint flakes from the bathroom wall. The wastebasket's full. The toilet drips. The man from La Mirada wears his jacket. "I come downtown every week," he says as we step into a bathroom stall. Maybe thinking of Elkins, the ticket-window man drops in after a while. "No pass outs, remember," he says to me.

I bet some of the people who used this bathroom during the Golden Age of Hollywood have performed onstage here, too.

"I myself was in the Navy," the man says.

When he inspects the floor to see whether it's dry so near the dripping toilet, I think of Ma telling me over and over, "God's holy body is not to be marred by man." I say this out loud to Joey, say it to Fatty Arbuckle, to Jeff Chandler, to all who've been lonely. I hear the toilet running, feel the excitement building as Randolph Scott takes the stage. This is the old days in downtown L.A. "Dear Jesus," I say, as I think of the box office stars that may have stopped by. Now I'm the star of the midnight feature.

"Herbert," Joey says, as though he's getting closer to what he's looking for. "Herbert promised me he'd be here."

I wonder if it's the time to have the remaining guests step from behind the curtain on Ralph Edwards's show. What will they learn about Naked Adonis alone in the Golden State?

I don't know what to say to the teacher, fighting all that freeway traffic to be a guest on the program. What happens next, I don't get either, except that I'm fresh out of boot camp and don't understand life. I think of Ma and how we'll watch Ralph Edwards together when I'm home next year. The happiness George Gobel and Lucille Ball find will bring tears to my mother's eyes. I'll hug her and tell her I love her and don't cry it's only a TV show.

Tonight in L.A., I'm on an episode of *This Is Your Life*. As Joey helps me become a nudist, I think of how we're being filmed before a live audience. Anyone could walk in here. Then I don't think of anything. My mind and body grow numb with the same pleasure Willa once brought me.

"Better put your clothes on," Joey says.

"Sorry I don't know Herbert," I say.

"I'll keep looking," he says.

When we leave the men's room, he winks as though I'll be coming back to see him. The men stare at us. A couple walks toward the bathroom. If I was home, I'd shovel the snow my dad wrote about in the letter. I'd plead with Willa to stay with me.

"Are *you* Herbert?" Joey's asking people.

Halfway up the aisle, a moviegoer says, "Why'd you put on your clothes? Don't go. It's early."

Joey asks him the Herbert question.

Famous now, I tell the moviegoer, "I'm Adonis."

When I make it to the back of the theater and push open the lobby door, Private Elkins is at the ticket window asking about me. "Don't pay to come in! I'm okay, Elkins," I tell him. "Don't come looking. This is *my* life. Let's go," I say, trying to protect him from the movies.

He's already purchased his ticket. When I tell him I've been waiting for him, he wonders why I'm not wearing my shirt and jacket, only my T-shirt with the sleeves rolled up to show off the tattoo. "What happened in there?" he asks.

"It was hot," I say, wondering whether he wants to be a celebrity.

When we walk out, it's freezing. California isn't supposed to be this way. Beneath the marquee advertising *Ten Days in a Nudist Camp* and the other movies, he says he's angry with me for leaving earlier. "Now I've bought another ticket."

"I told you not to. I'll pay you for it and throw it away," I tell Elkins. "It's cold," I say. I put on my shirt.

This is where Ralph Edwards comes in again, when Elkins is look-ing at me like I'm not the person he remembers. Mr. Edwards walks up to me with the microphone.

"Al Bronkowski, still nineteen-years-old," Mr. Edwards says, "you've been surprised by who's come onstage. One by one, they've walked out until there you were, surrounded by new friends and old. The teacher from La Mirada, the ticket-window man, your other friends. We want them to share your memories, so each will receive a book of photographs from tonight's program. Al Bronkowski, on a cold night you walked down the aisle of a movie theater in down-town Los Angeles, and now you'll have these memories to cherish. Al Bronkowski, Golden Boy, Naked Adonis. This Is Your Life!"

WHO IS BRONISŁAW SLINKER?

An immigrant, he came to the United States under the Displaced Persons Act of 1948. Then under the Louisiana Resettlement Program, he worked like other Polish immigrants on sugarcane plantations in the South. Also, like many Poles, Mr. Slinker lives in the East End neighborhood of Superior, Wisconsin, near the Bronkowskis, the Urbaniaks, and the Pogozalskis.

What does he do here, or what did he do here before retirement? A laborer, Mr. Slinker continued writing his stories as he worked on the waterfront. The stories have appeared in Polish journals. A Loyola University of Chicago professor, Dr. John Merchant, has written about Mr. Slinker in "An Outpost of Polishness . . . *Placówka polskości*," published in *Rocznik Komparatystyczny* (University of Gdańsk), the "outpost" being our neighborhood. A Polish professor, Dr. Sonia Caputa, has written about Mr. Slinker in the journal *Wielkie tematy literatury amerykańskiej . . . Great Themes in American Literature* (University of Silesia) and elsewhere. An interview with Mr. Slinker titled "*Pisząc spłacam dług Bogu . . .* By Writing I Serve My God" appeared in *Arcana* (Kraków) along with his story "*Pani* Burbul."

You could say Mr. Slinker is a ghost writer, more precisely a ghost-haunted, ghostly writer in the East End of Superior, a figure no one but his translator knows. Because he's a white ethnic writer, he's pretty much voiceless in an American literature that prizes certain ethnic groups while neglecting others. It is hoped these fragments will change life for Mr. Slinker.

His "A Chance of Snow . . . *Sanza na Śnieg*" was published in *Akcent* (Lublin, Poland). The story concerns a seaman who, during the Solidarity Movement, leaves his ship when it comes to load grain in Superior. After living in this port city for a brief time, the yearning for his family's home in Gdańsk becomes great. Despite the political risk to him, Łukasz Cedzynski returns to the old country on another vessel that has put into port, taken on cargo, and is leaving. The Polish American family he's lived with is devastated, especially Agnieszka, the daughter.

Finding him gone, her parents, brother, and twelve-year-old Agnieszka search the town for him before heading to the docks. They call to a deckhand about Mr. Cedzynski, "Is he aboard?" At the place in "A Chance of Snow" when he doesn't come on deck to see them, the piece reads: "Statek jest ogromny. Komin I sterownia, liny i ładownie są prawie tak duże i wysokie jak elewator, z którego odpływa. . . . The ship is huge. The smokestack and wheelhouse, the cables, the hatch covers are almost as big and high as the elevator she's leaving.

"Except for the ship's name, *Ziemia Białostocka*, in white, the steel hull is black. At the top of the hull, white-and-green stripes run the ship's length; and, very high up on the bow, a Polish eagle, wings spread, is painted in white. Two harbor tugs move into position to guide the vessel from the slip. Sailors are hauling up the ladder. The hatches bang when the deckhands close them. Grain dust forms a yellow layer on the ice and snow. A sailor looks down from above the eagle . . ."

At the Aerial Lift Bridge in Duluth, Minnesota, a warning sounds that a ship's departing. The bridge rises. "We run through the cold as the ship turns into the entry. Pushing the channel ice up around her, the *Ziemia Białostocka* looks like a haunted dream of Poland in the night. . . . What is in Gdańsk that Mr. Cedzynski misses?" Agnieszka wonders.

Finally, weeks later when winter has truly set in, she tells herself, "I wish there was a place where a person could forget everything she's ever loved in life. That is my wish, which I know can never come true." As long as she can dream of the vessel's lights out in the ice, however, Łukasz Cedzynski is still with her.

Mr. Slinker has written all kinds of these stories. He is, as I say, an ethnic writer, though without a voice in American literature. Curiously, Mr. Slinker is becoming whiter and whiter. It has not helped that he's had to labor for many years in a lime plant in Superior, calcium hydroxide, lime, being a dry, white powder. He'd come home from work covered with it.

Where does Bronisław Slinker get his ideas? They come from close observation of this "outpost," the East End of Superior. For instance, there was once an old woman, a Pani Burbul, who walked in the cold by the Nemadji River in the East End. Polish boats also called regularly in our port during the Solidarity Era. An oil refinery still lights up the night over the East End. Mr. Slinker knows our lives and this ethnic outpost—perhaps better than we know them. Yet who knows Mr. Slinker?

One of his stories is called "A Dollar's Worth." If he isn't the boy in the story, Tomasz, and he couldn't possibly be, then where could he have gotten the idea? Well, the story is about me, Malinowski, his translator. I told him the story. In a way, Mr. Slinker has translated my life into Polish for me to translate back into English. The story is a testament to Mr. Slinker's imagination. I have known him forty years.

A DOLLAR'S WORTH

A story written in Polish by Bronisław Slinker.
Translated by Tomasz Malinowski.

When I was eight, I had no money to buy presents for my family. Where would I get money? For Christmas, my twelve-year-old sister would buy me a present from her allowance. My grandmother in America and my parents bought us clothes and toys. Katarzyna received a doll and a doll house, and I received a cardboard box of Lincoln Logs and a toy truck. Another year, Katarzyna got a book, *The Wizard of Oz.*

We'd open the gifts after having the *Wigilia* supper with my mother's side of the family. Grandmother Fronckiewicz prepared the meal. After Grandfather's death, she lived with my Uncle Augie near the lumberyard. The first star in the sky guided us to her in the South End neighborhood of our town of twenty-six thousand.

On such a holy night, aunts, uncles, and cousins waited for us. We had to go three miles to see them, but we couldn't leave till my dad had stopped at the tavern for a beer, then cleaned up at home. At the flour mill, he stacked sacks of durum wheat and semolina flour onto pallets that would be loaded into boxcars on the spur track.

On the main floor of this flour mill, a man-lift, "the Humphrey," rattled up and down. To ride to another floor, a mill hand took a foot- and handhold on the wood blocks attached to the leather belt. As it rose through an opening on each floor, the worker pressed himself to the man-lift as he might later press himself to his wife at night.

On the engine room floor where the Humphrey began its jour- ney was another belt that spun around two cylindrical drums thirty feet apart. Once, a cat was caught on the belt. Another time, an employee fell one story down the man-lift. After my dad had worked the Christmas Eve day shift, he was done with the place.

Once all of the families arrived at Augie's, he served the grown- ups a glass of wine. Then we shared a wafer with the manger scene stamped on it. The wafer is called *opłatek* and is part of the custom in which you exchange a piece of wafer with another person and he or she with you. Another part of the custom requires straw be placed on the table to recall the manger setting. By now, it was dark outside and maybe snowing.

There being only enough space in the dining room for the grown- ups, the children stayed in the adjoining living room. When the adults kneeled around the table, we kneeled. It was odd watching them, normally so familiar to us, become distant as they prayed in a language some of my cousins didn't hear much at home. Even the ones who knew a little Polish were surprised how serious the adults became around Grandmother Fronckiewicz's table on this evening of the year. If you've not heard it, the Polish language sometimes sounds like it's whispered. As we listened, my relatives whispered prayers from a thousand years ago.

After the Wigilia supper, Grandmother gave each child a silver dollar. During the car ride home, I'd keep the silver dollar warm the way it'd felt from her hand. As long as it stayed warm, I felt close to her.

Later, after my sister and I had opened our presents, I still felt Grandmother close to me. When I was just starting to feel I couldn't disappoint my father—a feeling I got on Christmas Eve and on my birthday but never other times—he asked, "Didn't you get us any- thing? You could've bought your sister something at least."

I didn't know what to say. What could I do without money? How could I enjoy my own presents when he'd made me feel this way?

Getting up from the paper and boxes littering the floor, the new shirt and pajamas, the tin soldiers, I went to the buffet in the dining room where I'd hidden Grandmother's gift. Presenting it to my father, I wondered if maybe he'd felt helpless at the mill working eight or ten hours with nobody to stand up for him. Now I was helpless. Though we were many years apart in age, my father and I had helplessness in common.

To this day, I repeat to myself what he'd said to me that night. Its meaning depends on which word I emphasize. "I don't *want* that!" it will sometimes sound like, or "I *don't* want that!," or "I don't want *that!*" Everything was off-kilter. When I'd tried giving him the silver dollar, he'd said, "I don't want that!"

My heart froze. I decided that when I went upstairs to bed, I'd place the silver dollar under my father's pillow. If he wouldn't accept it from my hand, then this method of giving it to him would please him when he found the coin. I could go to sleep knowing that in the morning he'd be happy. I'd be the boy who never failed him. In Polish, the diminutive form of *Tomasz* is *Tomaszu*. When my father used it in the morning, it would show he loved me, Tomasz Malinowski.

To save on the heat, we kept the dampers closed on the heat registers upstairs. Of course, the silver dollar would get cold. Maybe it would be 2 a.m. when he discovered it under his pillow. Maybe he'd return to his peaceful dreams. I don't know that I've slept so soundly as I did after giving my father the silver dollar.

At daybreak, I went downstairs certain he'd be happy. But he said nothing about the dollar. A couple of days later, I was waiting for him to say something when he told me to empty the ashes from the furnace. A week later, he'd still said nothing about the gift. Not a glimmer of acknowledgment. It was like the dollar was payment on a debt I owed him.

I remember my visits to the flour mill. The huge belt that spun around the cylindrical drums terrified me. So did the man-lift that never stopped going from floor to floor. I remember that at home I could never understand my father. I recall his saying about the silver dollar I received from Grandmother Fronckiewicz, "I don't want that," when I think what he meant was, "I don't want you, Tomaszu."

Perhaps I've missed something in translating this from Polish to English. While sitting at his kitchen table, I'd first told Mr. Slinker my story. Now I will implore him to please return to it to see whether part of the story has been misinterpreted, mistranslated. Maybe there's something that's been left out, something I could have said differently to my father, something he could have said to me.

Otherwise, the story will end with my father always saying, "I don't want you, Tomaszu."

THE BLONDES OF WISCONSIN

The beautiful blonde is pointing at you from the poster. HEY, YOU AT THE URINAL SHAKING THE TINY THING IN YOUR FINGERS, TINY TIM. ARE YOU MAN ENOUGH FOR US? On a poster taped to the back bar in the tavern, another poster warns, YOU'RE TOAST, NUMB NUTS! A third poster reads, HEY, YOU-BIG-FAT-SLOB-SUCKING-ON-THE-32-OUNCE-CAN-OF-BEER, PREPARE TO FIGHT THE WOMAN OF YOUR DREAMS. The posters hit you in living color. Are you going to be near Dodgeville, Viroqua, Union Grove, Beaver Dam? Stop in if you want your butt kicked.

Gentlemen, meet the Blondes of Wisconsin: Mardi Morgan, Sun Prairie, 125 lbs. Once changed oil at a Quick Lube. Fed up with the job, she drained a guy's crankcase, told him his car was good-to-go, then left for Madison to hit the heavy bag at the West Side Y. Betty Dooley, Janesville, 132 lbs. Worked two jobs to support the bum she lived with. When he told her to get a third job, she punched him out. Sonny Martini, Baraboo, 140 lbs. Always had problems with men. Loretta Simons, Donna Sue Gustafson, Judy Knudsen—they're blondes. And the author of this tome? I'm a redhead, Etheline, named after my grandmothers Ethel and Adeline.

Carla Johnson's the boss. I've been with her forever. On mild days when we're leaving a town and she's feeling up to it, Carla sits in a chaise lounge watching us load the equipment trailer. In the parking lot, she directs us with great flourishes. "Don't forget the turnbuckles," she'll say, words coming like punch combinations. "Remember the water bottles." *Pow*. "Remember what you did to that fat guy in Hustisford with your overhand right." *Bam*. In the Come-On-In Tavern, Patch Grove, Wisconsin, where we'll break down the ring after a few hours' rest, we kicked serious ass last night.

Now it's midnight, Thursday, March 19 in a year that doesn't matter. In nearby Prairie du Chien, we've encouraged the motel manager to move us to the bug-free rooms. A week earlier in the only motel in Richland Center, a section of our door had been missing. To keep the mice from saying goodnight in person, we'd said, "Fix it," to the owner. There was no misunderstanding our request. A week before in this Red Oak, Wisconsin, "hot sheet" place, there was nothing in the parking lot but our van, our equipment trailer with the boxing ring, and someone's black Cadillac. When I complained to the boss that whoever'd stayed here the night before needed Beano, she said, "It's something in the vents." When the smell finally got to her, she changed her mind. "Tell the guy at the desk to move us," she told me. If you're a desk clerk in Nowhereville, wouldn't you listen when eight tough dames stop to visit? This was before we met the champion up north, the contender who came back for one last fight. In his prime, the guy had been a boxer named Ed Bronkowski.

Before telling you about him, I should confess that I enjoy writing about the girls and that Carla has a problem with Xanax, Valium, anything we can get for her in the bars. She lives for pills. No matter if they're blue, green, red, or multicolored, she'll pop them. When Carla's in La La-Land, I write about the roadside diners, run-down motels, and other places the girls endure. My notes read:

"35.2 miles from Verona to Brodhead."

"The corn in Walworth County looked good last summer."

"Sonny's twin sister Bunny works at the Circus World Museum in Baraboo and will join us in June."

I jotted this yesterday:

"What does it mean to have a good heart?"

"The Blondes of Wisconsin . . . a good way to make a living."

When she straightens out for a few hours, Carla, who's put this enterprise together over five years, tells us where we're going next. Darkness under her eyes, hands fidgeting, she says, "In Green Bay, it's pronounced 'Al-o-way.' Up north, it's, 'Al-o-weez.' That's where the bar is that we're working. First, we'll enter the Itasca neighborhood of Superior, then the Allouez neighborhood. 'Al-o-weez.' It sounds like someone with COPD choking on ore dust, 'Al-o-wheeze' like a person's last breaths will be spent trying to explain the place to outsiders. You might've noticed my emphysema when I talk about it. I tried living there, but things went wrong," Carla will say on and on in anticipation of our trip.

Having noted her observations about a highway in that port city, a highway that passes so close to houses we'll see couples quarreling over supper, here are more details. When the girls enter the ring in some dive, the men go nuts. They aren't bad guys usually, but we can do without the bitter ones. Thank Heavens, the Blondes have been instructed by Duke Lynch, boxing trainer and corner man in Madison. He'd worked with the girls for a year before they went on the road, lots of running, jumping rope, shadow boxing, sit-ups, long arm drills, sparring. Duke would get in the ring with them. "Let men ogle you," he always told the girls. "If they're eyeing you, they're not boxing."

Now Carla enters the picture in my notes and observations. I'm writing an exposé of three hearts, one of them mine. By "the heart," I mean the place which allows us to understand and help others, to love and sympathize with them when they need us. This may sound strange given our line of work, but Heart Number One in this exposé belongs to Carla. In her white tuxedo, she'll nod to a bartender to cue Pat Benatar's "Hit Me with Your Best Shot" as she says into the microphone, "Who wants to fight a lady?" She'll be in this corner, in that corner. She'll lean over the ropes, yell at the crowd to get them going. Poynette, Footville, Cuba City, Westby. We've been all over southern

Wisconsin with her. Wauzeka, Wautoma, Wauwatosa, Waukesha. We've crossed the Rock, the Pecatonica, and the Kickapoo rivers. We've seen the Mississippi a hundred times.

To antagonize the men of Superior, which is *way* up north, Carla's going to wear a full-length coat you won't find in the hinterlands. Imagine on a mature lady of sixty-something a quilted, calf-length, lilac-colored coat. Yes, lilac-colored! Lilacs in the cold Wisconsin spring! Imagine the reaction Carla will get from the barflies in Souptown, aka Superior. The HEY, YOU AT THE URINAL poster is probably already riling them up. After a long day on a bulldozer at the landfill, some guy is probably thinking what he'd do to the girl calling him "Numb Nuts" and threatening him with her fists. But this is for two nights from now.

As for this March night, it's Carla, me, and the Blondes in Prairie du Chien. I fluff up her pillows, relax her with a pill. The coconut-scented air freshener in the room freshens nothing. When I remind her that I've been with the Blondes a long time, telling her this out of love and gratitude, she says I should emcee. For months, she's asked me to take over. If I agree, I can wear the tuxedo and the white patent leather shoes. I can run the show the way I want. She'll raise the girls' pay, too. It'll be great, she says. Though her mind's going everywhere tonight, she seems to mean it more than the other times. "I'll never sleep," she's saying one minute, the next singing a song she'd last heard on Pulaski Day in a polka town: "*Tick-tick-tick tock, goes the clock on the wall . . .*" When I massage her hands, her fingers, and tell her she'll be okay, she says again, "You do it, Etheline. Run the show. You're young. Get us a TV contract. I can't work. The late nights and noise are too much."

Finally, at 5 a.m., she drifts off. I realize what's happened. Four years after joining her, I've been promoted to CEO. I love her for this. I love the girls. I want her business to grow. Despite our occasional complaints, the girls and I make out fine. We get paychecks, bonuses, motel rooms that are often nice. The show's been run by a beautiful lady. Under the mascara and false lashes are eyes that have trusted others all her life. She's cared for the hurt and helpless, which at one time was every one of us in the Blondes of Wisconsin.

On the best nights, they take out their frustrations and mine with a solid blow to a guy's chin. It's a good way to stay physically fit. Then in the morning, we store the floorboards, turnbuckles, and other items in the trailer. This time, we're saying adieu to Prairie du Chien, "the Prairie of the Dogs," and driving a long way to hook up with Interstate 94 then Wisconsin 53 so that the boss can go to her old home the way she'd left it. It makes no sense to travel out of the way, but that's her wish. She's obsessed with Superior.

We rest in Bloomer. Carla gets high. I leave her in the room with the TV on to go see the girls. Betty gives me a chair. Donna Sue rests on the bed. Mardi and Sonny lean against the wall.

Done heating her curling iron, Judy says, "How's the boss?" then jokes about being in bloomers in Bloomer.

"Whatever's bothering you, don't let it. I've been promoted to management. The news just broke."

"Promoted by who?"

"The boss."

"What's it mean to us?" the girls ask.

"Big raises for all of you. Carla'd never let you down," I say.

They puzzle over this. They talk together in a corner of the room.

"We know she wouldn't," Mardi finally says.

"The good life just got better," Sonny exults as the girls cheer and slap my back.

"Vroom-vroom Etheline!" Judy says as we go to Carla's room where the boss makes it look as though her decision to step down was mine and the girls'. "So, you figured out I need help. *Viva la revolución!*" she says. She's seen the phrase spray-painted on buildings in college towns. The girls use it as our motto.

"Don't fade out on us, Carla. You're still our boss," we say. "You're a silent partner now."

With her knowing we love her and that she'll be able to rejoin us when she's better, Carla tries to rest, but she's high. "Put some quarters in the slot, Etheline. I need a Magic Fingers Massage," she says.

The night's a blur for us after the announcement. I look over travel plans, contract obligations, the posters I'll have to mail. I've been preparing for this. When you learn the routine, you get to know a business. During a spare moment, I write about the boss, "Beautiful gal! Tall, elegant!" Then other notes:

"Transfer of power."

"Carla very, very tired. Rehab a necessity."

"Northern Wisconsin, here we come!"

Last night, a two-Xanax night in Bloomer, we got business straightened out. Carla's better in the morning. Knowing she's going to detox, she can look to a future with us after she's clean. On the trip north, the boss talks about the town, its ore docks, taverns, grain elevators. "Superior's got roughly twenty-six thousand people living in a 55.65 square mile area. That's only two square miles less than Minneapolis. The woods and fields go on forever. You'll see. It's a great, rusted city, too, lots of rundown buildings, empty storefronts, but like me it's rising from the ashes. 'Superior—One Great Lake and a Whole Lot More! Superior—Where Rail Meets Sail!'" she says, parroting Chamber of Commerce slogans.

The highway we come in on merges with the one from Ashland and the U.P. of Michigan. Twenty miles from Superior, the billboards start. DREAMLAND SUPPER CLUB. THE PRESIDENT'S BAR & LIQUOR STORE. Then there's the town she loves, part of it obscured by industrial smoke. Highway 2/53 becomes East Second Street. Though it does little good, a flashing light warns: NO SPEEDING. What a place! The houses are four feet from the curb. Traffic flies past. Dust and newspapers blow down the streets. People quarrel in windows.

The bar stands near a squealing belt that hauls taconite from an inland facility, through a neighborhood, then out to a dock. It's a mile-and-a-half journey. The beige-colored tin encasing the belt is red with the ore dust it was built to contain. A sign on the dust-streaked building below the belt reads, "Clean Out Pit #4." According to a sign in the parking lot, tonight's event, "The Bash by the Belt," is cosponsored by the Whoop 'n Holler Tavern and a beer distributor.

Setting up the ring takes time. Into the bar, the girls carry the joists, the floorboards, the canvas that will cover the floor, the turnbuckles and ring ropes, the stools and boxing gloves. The sweat inside the gloves is still drying from two nights ago. Day drinkers stare at the TV. Other patrons talk sports with the bartender, play cribbage at a corner table. In her lilac coat, Carla adds color to the place.

"Ammo's around somewhere," the bartender says. When his boss comes up with a pony keg from the cold basement, we see Ammo's ugly face. It has skin tags all over it. When he removes his jacket, we see them on his neck. The cool, musty basement maybe encourages their growth. Before he turns off the light down there and shuts the door, we feel the dank air in the bar. Ammo's belly stretches his polo shirt.

"Who's tonight's headliner?" we ask him once we introduce ourselves.

"He's a crowd pleaser that thinks he's fighting for a title. It's good fun."

"We don't want our girl hurt, right, Etheline?" Carla says. "You'll guarantee us the headliner guy's okay?"

"It's all fun," Ammo says. "Don't worry. He's been around here all winter. He lives with his ma. Says he's working himself into shape. I suppose he could be. I seen him jog by. This is his big chance. He's a pretty good guy. I hear he was on the *H.L. Stimson* but was a liability with his head messed up like it is. He was in the ring once. Don't worry. He's harmless now."

But who *is* Judy fighting? Ammo could be telling us anything, Carla and I think. We can't risk any of the girls.

"We're ready," they say when the ring's up and we head to the Androy Hotel to rest and prepare for the night.

As Carla paces in her room, sits for a while, then jumps up to pace again, she says, "I wanted to see Superior. But you go out there for me and do a good job." She looks from the fourth-floor window, checks the clock. "'Next to Duluth, We're Superior!'" she says.

"I get it, Carla," I say. After this first slogan, she asks for a pill. "Half a pill!" I tell her as I slip into her clothes.

"Things go unregulated in life, Etheline," she says, as if trying to understand what's worn her down. An older version of us, she's preparing the Blondes to fight the way she's fought most of her life. When guys did bad things to her, she gave it back to them. Carla never cowered. Her heart got bigger along the way. Despite her own suffering, she was kind to anyone who needed it, gave to every cause, to the girls and me most recently. Now her heart is slowing down.

"We're not buying you pills anymore. I hated doing that," I tell her.

"It's my fault I got undisciplined like this," she says.

"What?" I ask her. But the Blondes in the hall tell me it's time to go. She doesn't talk now anyway. She wants me to get started in business. Who knows the heart's secrets? Why did she invite me to join her when we met in Beloit? She knew I had part-time jobs and bills. I marvel over what she's done for me. Carla Johnson's heart is a mystery that will never be understood. I've seen her love and aid so many, men *and* women, waitresses, truck drivers. Maybe she began giving in before she'd started the Blondes. This is a heart that's given and given. The lessons of it send me into the night.

If I can say these things about Carla Johnson, I can say them about the place she loves. There must be *something* here. Superior is deflated, post-industrial, hoping tourism will lead it forward. "'Superior—Living Up to Our Name!'" Carla makes me say before I leave. Somewhere down these boulevards and elm-lined streets, I imagine beauty, a stone fountain, a hedge of wild roses. I dream of a white seaplane in a blue sky above a blue bay, July air so perfect it restores every belief you have in summer. This must be the way Superior is in Carla's mind.

A block from the belt on *this* dreary night eighty-nine days before summer, we hear the laughing and yelling. There are two hundred people lined up for "the Bash." The red dust falls. The belt squeals.

The half-pint Sonny fights is drunk. Betty, Loretta, Donna Sue, and Mardi win their bouts. They leave their opponents with bruised egos, a bloody nose, a shiner. In the meantime, a pickled pig's foot glances off of a white tuxedo. Someone flicks a cigarette butt into the ring. *Oh, Carla, if you could see me doing this for you.*

Fifteen-minute intermissions become thirty minutes so that Ammo can sell more beer. He has things roaring. He keeps the beer and liquor sales. Carla gets the gate. The girls and I are going to do well tonight. When our headliner throws off her fur coat—part of the glamor of the Blondes of Wisconsin—the crowd yells so loud I bet Carla can hear it in her room. When he sees her, Ammo's eyes bug out. With Pat Benatar singing on the jukebox, here I am, High Octane Etheline, "Vroom Vroom," standing beside the most beautiful blonde in Wisconsin.

Part Swedish, part Norwegian, she's a milk drinker, Judy Knudsen. She stands close to six feet tall. She has good genes but has had a terrible life—the usual story, a broken home, men with no money that didn't treat her right. Carla took her in. On travel days, Judy shadow boxes, does push-ups and sit-ups, tries to get in her roadwork. Her blonde braids pinned in circles behind her head, she beams out at the bar crowd. When the bout starts, she'll wear a mouthpiece to protect her sparkling teeth.

To calm the prefight jitters, she raises a foot off the canvas, lowers it, raises the other one. Over and over, she does this as she taps her gloves together.

"Who's up next?" I yell to Ammo.

"The sailor I told you about. He's changing," he says, happy with the night so far. "He's in the men's room. Here, he's coming out now! Let him through!"

The guy spots me in the ring. When he sees Judy, he looks away, as if he's never had a beautiful woman waiting for him. His gray T-shirt was white once. To keep his pants up, he has a leather belt with a big buckle like a cowboy might've donated to Goodwill. When one of the girls holds open the ropes, he climbs through, jogs across the ring. The back of his robe says Ed "the Bronko" Bronkowski.

It's a setup. Ammo knows it. I know it. The guy is to take a beating in front of two hundred people so that Ammo's patrons can whoop and holler. I've seen men pretend to be knocked out, seen them unlace the eighteen-ounce boxing gloves with their teeth and run away. The Blondes have an unusual effect on men. In this case, we worry about elder abuse. On the other hand, a man can surprise you. This one's a little scary. Part of his face should be here, part there. The two halves of his misery don't match up. Still, there's something earnest and noble in his face. The crowd laughs at him. In the blue corner, a ring-card girl holds up a sign that says THE BRONKO'S STALL. Then Ammo points to me and says, "Let's get ready to rumble."

Imagine a guy in a gray T-shirt and polyester pants. I don't know *what* he wears on his feet, old sneakers of some sort. He manages to answer the bell in them. Judy takes a jab, shakes it off. It's like this Ed is doing something he's practiced for years but is bewildered by it. Early on, when Judy slips to a knee, the crowd yells. I know the guy didn't connect. After an exchange of punches, she'd lost her footing.

The Bronko takes a breath, slaps his head with a glove to keep focused. On a face like his, it's hard to find clues of anything. Ammo said the Bronko's sailed the lakes. Maybe he's been a custodian in his life, a dishwasher, maybe a bum who rides trains out of this city and back. He's been somewhere not many of us have gone.

When Judy signals she's okay thirty seconds into the round, we tell her, "Throw your combinations. Don't let him off." She hooks off her jab, jabs off her hook. The crowd yells, "*Bronko! Bronko!*" Who knows what the guy remembers? Maybe he thinks of all the times he's been hit. Maybe he just wants to snap off a good jab, to keep his shoulder up when he does. He's good for a round, for two rounds, three, until his punches appear to stop working.

There's shape and then there's boxing shape. Looking as though he's been banged around all his life, he's managed three good rounds with a beauty from Port Washington. A guy can look like this and still give her a workout. The night's over, though. Once Ammo cuts our check, we're gone. Judy thinks the Bronko's done, too. She looks at us. In the instant I tell her, "Watch him. He's got something left—," the uppercut slams upward between her forearms and elbows. In slow motion, we see enough padding and leather to numb you, to break your nose.

It's been a year since she's been hit. She drops her gloves. My heart sinks when her legs go. The crowd gets noisier as she wobbles about, hangs on the ropes. We fall for it. When she turns around to face me, I'm ready to throw in the towel until she does this theatrical thing. Like it's something from *Love Story* or some other sappy movie, she throws him a kiss. The arc of her hand goes out a good distance toward him. She did this in Cazenovia once.

When the Bronko, captivated by her, stumbles over, she grabs the microphone. As if the crowd noise is incidental, you can hear her perfectly. The only thing that matters in the bar now is an old song, a Siren's song. Who sang this? *"Fly me to the moon, let me play among the stars, let me see what spring is like on Jupiter and Mars."* Fascinated by the song, the Bronko stops at center ring. He implores her for something. Love? Pity? The warmth of sentiment in a cold world? All of us want that.

Then she nails him. This sounds crazy, but he's last seen between Jupiter and Mars. I wonder how it is out there, whether he's happy traveling. He's gone far enough for us to be concerned. When he reenters earth's atmosphere, he lands on the canvas. Looking more comfortable on his back than he was standing up, he rests a hand over his heart. The heart again. Always the heart. I slide his robe out of the ring.

When I raise Judy's hand in victory, Ed's entourage takes off. The Bronko sits up. He must know he's given us a good show. A few people don't like the way things have turned out. This big guy who's bragged about filling potholes for the Highway Department blocks our way. Everything gets jumbled when the girls swing at him. We could tear the place apart if we had thirty Blondes. With the bartender and owner calming things, someone calls the cops. More people head for the exits.

On the street, lights flashing, I tell the police. "You better call an ambulance."

They radio this in; they write things down. There's no need for High Octane Etheline to explain more.

"Do we have our things?" I ask the girls.

"We killed it," Betty says.

Upstairs in the hotel, I visit them again. "How are you?"

"We're fine. A few scrapes."

When I go to Carla's room, she asks how it went. "Did you survive without me?"

I tell her about everything. "Can I show you how I moved, Carla? I did it like you would. I imitated you. Because you're our teacher, the Blondes and I did a great job."

I point toward each part of the room as though we're in the Whoop 'n Holler. For one night, I was the fuel that runs the Blondes. "Are you ready, Carla? *Are you ready!?* Watch this. I was you more than you," I tell her when I see her smiling as she drifts into a wonderland where we're the team of girls she loves.

That's my Carla. Come to town. Do what you have to. Now face rehab. Despite the drunks and pothole fillers that have stood in her way all these years, she's made a life for herself. From humble beginnings as a carhop, hotel maid, or whatever she did to the top of the fight game in cities like Lynxville and Eastman.

I dim the lights, remove the patent leather shoes. Then I hear knocking down the hall. Someone's saying, "You can't be up here." When I peek out, I see the night clerk steering a fellow toward the elevator. "Bring him here," I say. It's Ed Bronkowski, who had his last fight on the night the snow in Soup-town started as drizzle.

I try not to look at him. There's no telling a story from that kind, broken face. "I need to go somewhere," he's saying, his voice softer than I expected, as if one day it might fade into silence.

"Look who's here, Carla," I say. "He thinks we're his ticket out."

"I like his looks," Carla says. "We should give him a job."

I suppose we could hire him to rinse the spit bucket and break down the ring. He looks like he'd be up for that. We could plant him on a stool in Rhinelander. The rule of thumb at the Five-Knuckle Tavern, like at most places on weekend nights in Wisconsin, is "Stumble out, two steps, and a heave." The patrons would see the look in his eyes. They'd believe him when he said, "I fought the Blondes of Wisconsin. Look at the posters on the wall. The Blondes are coming here next. Have you seen my wife? She's in Milwaukee, no, Cudahy! Tell her to call me. Or in case of emergency, call Bronisław Slinker, Mrs. Pogozalski, or anyone in Superior."

Maybe after Rhinelander, once people have had enough of the Ed Bronkowski Experience, we'll go to the Door Peninsula or Marinette; or we'll turn the van south to Antigo or southwest to Medford. We'll get him to the suburbs of Milwaukee; but before we put him on a barstool there, we'll train him to say, "Hi! My Name's Stud." He'll be a greeter. Joe Louis in Vegas. Chuck Wepner in Bayonne. Right now, he's lonely. A kiss will restore him, give him hope. Freely given, a kiss tells the recipient that in another's life she or he is worth something. That's how Carla kissed me when I told her we were getting her to rehab.

Maybe I'm wrong about this Ed guy. He might just be a quiet man who doesn't want a job. Maybe he'd like to tag along, though, see some new places in the Dairy State. If we hire a greeter, we'll need subs if the girls get hurt. This is High Octane Etheline, Heart Number Two in the exposé, in action. Think Big! That's my motto. If our recruits—say, a twenty-year-old from Fort Atkinson, a divorcée from Cedarburg—aren't blondes or don't box, we'll bleach 'em and teach 'em. With Carla in rehab, maybe Duke will leave Madison to join us. An ex-pug, Duke is sympathetic to us. Who'd dare stop us then, eight blondes, or ten or fifteen of us with the entourage of the Duke, Ed Bronkowski, and the new hires I'm planning for? Then I realize this is crazy.

"Goodnight," I whisper to Carla. All this time, Ed Bronkowski, Heart Number Three, is saying, "What time does the bus leave?"

"It's gone. The bus has left for Milwaukee. However, I've got a place you can wait for the next one. Right here. I've got your ticket," I say.

With Carla high on pills, I go to him. Through the window, I see the March snow, the wind picking up. Where does a contender wander when he's lost the main event? In his condition, I can't let him out on a night like this. He was brave. He had heart. He had a nice face once. He can rest here. In the morning, I'll give him money to tide him over. A man like this, a thankful man, is worth the trouble. Strong hearts, good hearts are everywhere in the world, and he has one. It's like Carla's.

From here on, people can say what they want about the Blondes of Wisconsin. That's their right. But it's also my right to tell them that the last words I speak as I turn off the lights and go to my own room are *"Viva la revolución!"*

"Viva la revolución!" Carla whispers to me; and the old man, tagging after me, says it, grateful that he's found people in the world that will care for him.

THE VOCABULARY LESSON

Sober for a few days, my Uncle Al is driving the car. Mr. Slinker sits in front with him, Keith and I in back. Because of Mr. Slinker's putting in a good word for him, my brother's gotten part-time work at the lime plant. He needs the money to finish school. I'll be attending college in Superior next year, too. Now we're going to see my Uncle Ed at his home in the country.

Ed's nickname is "the Bronko." He's one of the guys like Mr. Jens Carlsgard or Mr. Emil Erickson staring at the tile floor of the Middle River Health and Rehabilitation facility, the Memory Care Unit, and saying, "Tell Sally to come get me."

Day after day, the nurse tells Jens Carlsgard, "Shh—You have no Sally. You have a son. He's in Oregon. You're outside of Superior, Wisconsin."

"Okeydokey," my Uncle Ed always pipes up from his wheelchair, though the nurse isn't speaking to him but to Jens Carlsgard about the Sally who Jens and Uncle Ed mistake for their daughter.

The men have joined a club that doesn't use many words. I'm the one interested in words. The old men at Middle River are Jens, Emil, Ernie, Gust, Casper. They are in their seventies, I'd bet. Compared to them, my uncle is young.

"A prizefighter gets paid for what he does, right, Uncle Al?" I ask. "Ed got paid for getting beat up, right?"

"Look up the word 'punchy,'" Al says.

"'Groggy. Dazed. Suffering cerebral injury and bleeding from blows received in prizefighting,'" I read off of my phone.

"What's a 'punching bag?'" Al asks.

"'A usually inflated, suspended bag to be punched for exercise or training in boxing,'" my brother says.

"Good. Like your uncle was a punching bag," Al says. "We'll get in a quick visit."

On this afternoon in early December, everything's slate colored on the hills in Duluth and in the lowlands where we're driving. From Superior, it's an eighteen-mile trip past forests and fields to Middle River. I think Ed's mind must be like the gray fog rising from Lake Superior.

At least a welcoming light shines from the buildings. That's good to see. The place smells like the meal the patients have had for lunch. It's hot inside. Fans blow in the hallway. When we spot Ed, he's staring at his hands like they're holding a dragonfly or a butterfly. His chin rests on his chest. I wonder if the butterfly appeared after he got hit in one of his bouts. Uncle Al has a newspaper clipping from the *Omaha World-Herald* that says Ed sat on the stool between the eighth and ninth rounds and threw up. After that, he had a sickness in his brain nobody reported to the boxing commission, not Butch Maeder, his manager, not the doctor at ringside. This is the result: my uncle with a blanket on his lap, waiting for the timer's bell to signal the next round.

Out in the hallway, Ed still wears his stained bib from lunch. He doesn't look right. If he spots you in the Memory Care Unit and you back away from him, he'll holler, "Hey!"

One time when he'd spent the hour trying to recall who we were, he looked up from what occupied him. This was when he'd first come to Middle River, the same day we told Mr. Slinker where Ed was going to live. "It's good to see a friendly face," Ed whispered to me.

"What?" I'd asked, surprised he could speak. Then he must've thought, "I'm returning where I belong" because he didn't say anything more.

Now when we bring Ed into the room, he slumps in his wheelchair. Keith stares out the window. Al wears jeans, an old sweatshirt, a raggedy jacket. Tall and thin, Mr. Slinker stands quietly in a corner, gray coat draped over his shoulders. He must've looked like this in Warsaw many years ago.

"I have no idea where Ed's mind goes," Al says about his brother.

"In our sleep, do we live where he goes?" Keith asks.

"It's different where Ed is. We wake up. He never will," Al says.

This is how we talk in front of him. "What does the Bronko remember?" I ask them, wondering whether he's puzzling over how he got here when, in his mind, he was fighting great a week ago.

My Uncle Ed once taught me these three words. Maybe they were among the last hundred or two hundred words he knew. Just as strong winds push water to one side of a lake where it builds up, so had all the punches Ed took over the years built up on his brain. One of the words was "seiche." This is when water returns to the other side of the lake, the evening out of the surface of a body of water.

"Seiche," I say to him now from a distant shore. On this gray afternoon, I go on, "You taught me 'moonglade,' too. And 'scintillation.'"

He mumbles something.

"Do you remember 'scintillation,' the 'rapid changes in the brightness of a celestial body'? You wanted me to remember the words because you knew you couldn't."

There's still no response from him, never will be. After we stare at Ed for an hour, my Uncle Al says, "We gotta go."

When the nurse announces, "Emil, we're having cookies. You get ready for snacks, Ed and you other men," I hold Ed's hands. I don't like to hear old men cry in their rooms or in the hallway. It bothers me watching Ed picking at the loose threads on his blanket. The next time we visit, the threads will be there. One by one, Ed will be working to unravel them. Now, Mr. Slinker, who was a gentleman in the old country and a laborer in the United States, bows and says goodbye to my uncle.

Ms. Fanny Snowberg, my English teacher, and Mr. Slinker, the Polish writer, say I should be an author. Because of them, I spend time in the high school media center. I copy sentences from books, then following the same sentence structure, I rewrite them with information about Superior. My brother thinks it's silly. He's the one who's "off." A biology major, he's in great despair over his girlfriend. He's lost weight and can't eat. He asks me if I've seen her. He asks me if she's called. I have Mr. Slinker to guide me if my brother won't take me seriously. Mr. Slinker doesn't talk to many people, just to his translator and one or two others in the neighborhood. He liked my grandparents a lot, but they're gone now. We live in their old house. From my upstairs room, I can watch him writing and reading in *his* upstairs room. Sometimes I see him downstairs, his papers spread across a table, arguing over a word with Mr. Malinowski.

"Tell me about your neighborhood," Mr. Slinker said to me one day.

"It's your neighborhood, too," I said.

Instead of answering, he gave me a magazine with his story in it about an old woman displaced by World War Two. I've shown the story to Keith. Mr. Malinowski's translation begins: "Though everyone noted how well the old woman looked, Mrs. Burbul would reply 'Nic nie zkodzi . . . It doesn't matter' and go her way through the fields surrounding the [East End of Superior Wisconsin]. She went because the distances were very vast and wide and how you looked in God's eyes out there didn't matter—" In the Polish magazine *Arcana*, the story begins: "Choć wszyscy zauważali, że świetnie jak na swój wiek wygląda, Pani Burbul nieodmiennie odpowiadała—'Nic nie szkodzi'—po czym ruszała w dalszą drogę przez pola."

It struck me that Mr. Slinker had found someone or something to write about in the neighborhood. I thought nothing around here was worth it. Ms. Snowberg says that when I start my senior-year writing project for AP English, I must appeal to the senses. I have to show how the places that are known to us can be mysterious. I can write about Al, Ed, my brother Keith, the island I go to, everything. I'll think about it when I go out tonight, how Ed's had a hard life, how my other uncle drinks to forget Vietnam. Though Al returned safe from war, he never really came home. Ms. Snowberg says when I'm done with the project it will be my "epic." "It's already written in the stars or in some book of your life. It's out there. Go find it," she's said. As I prepare for later, I wish I could have her or Mr. Slinker with me.

A few hours after we've returned from Middle River, I go through the fields to the bay. The moon hangs like a cape over our neighborhood. Every sound of the dying earth is magnified. Leaves crunch, twigs snap off of branches when I pass.

A creek winds through a culvert beneath the Second Street viaduct. I hear it when I walk along the tracks then down a small hill to the bay. The island across the inlet is a half-mile long. A little west of it, an empty pier juts into the bay. East of the island rises the old Northern Pacific ore dock. Made of creosote-coated beams, it's huge. Pigeons nest in the ore pockets and rest on the steel chutes that are gradually being salvaged for scrap. East of it, past the Nemadji River, stand three more ore docks, only one in use.

Because it hasn't snowed yet this late in the fall, I've left no tracks on the way to Hog Island. Through the tag alder and brush on the lee side of the island, I see part of our neighborhood, the lighted window of my room, the lighted windows at Mr. Slinker's. Once you cross the island, which is mainly sand, some white birch, and a few pines, you get to the shore of the big bay, which extends from the St. Louis River estuary in Duluth all the way to the east side of Superior. The sandbar, the "Point" across from us, is in Minnesota. Foreign ships and "lakers" sail through the bay between Hog Island and Minnesota Point, then through the channel into Lake Superior. I can see the outline of the crumbling lighthouse, which was once the "zero starting point" for geodetic surveys of Lake Superior. I'm surveying this for Ms. Snowberg.

I scrape a place beside the ashes of a fire I made last week. I stack birchbark and kindling in the shape of a little house. When I add driftwood and the fire is going, I look up to see a lake boat passing dark and silent. Its running lights blend in with the lights on Minnesota Point, so that I barely see anything. Except for the sound of water piling up before the bow and the dull thrum of the propellers aft, the vessel goes secretively. Who on land besides me knows it's leaving?

I hear the fragile ice broken by the *Philip R. Clarke* wash ashore. When the weather turns really cold, the Coast Guard ice breaker will have to cut shipping lanes through the bay. Thankfully, the fire illuminates the shore. Sparks fly into the windless night when I throw on more driftwood. Inside the circle of light, I know where I am. When I walk outside the light, the fire looks different, as if something remains there when no one's near it. It's like a part of my consciousness or something stays by the fire. Another part looks back from the darkness. I think that when I return to the fire, I'll rejoin this consciousness. Knowing no one hears me, I call into the darkness to see what it's like to be alone. I call to my uncles, my brother. I wish Keith especially could answer. My brother's been heartbroken for months. I hope he's better tonight than he was this afternoon.

Soon, the fire will make patterns no will see. Because the inlet is sheltered and much smaller than the big bay, the ice is three or four inches thick. When I cross on the way home, the ice expands and contracts. I walk a few feet, slide a few. Though I know it's safe, I'm still frightened. When the ice heaves and groans, it seems like I'll never get off it. I wonder if the creaks and booms that roll over the inlet are like what Ed heard when blows shook his head in Omaha and he fell to the canvas. I pretend I'm there with him. The people in the arena are yelling for him to get up, but he can't. For a minute, it seems like all the ice is breaking. No matter how much I tell myself it's just the inlet expanding and contracting, the freezing of winter in the north, I run for it, forgetting about Ed for a minute.

From the shore, I look back at Hog Island. I'd been there for over two hours. The farther I've come from the island, the more isolated the fire. When I get to the top of the hill, I can see the orange flames. Something's left there of the person who built the fire, me, Andrew, *Andrzej* the high school student. On the way home, I talk aloud to Ed about the moon and the cold. I guide off the lighted window at Mr. Slinker's.

"Where's your brother?" my mother asks. "Didn't you go somewhere with him?"

"No," I tell her. "I'm frozen."

Upstairs, I think of the boat that went through the bay and out the entry. I think of Ed calling for his brother when Al's not there. Sometimes, we hear Ed yelling before we get to his floor at Middle River. The nurse says he does this at night, too. "Al! Al!"

Now my brother surprises me. He seems to come from nowhere. "Where've you been? I was worried about you," he says. Then he goes into his room across the hall so he can call his girlfriend. Though the door's closed, I hear him. I think he's asking her questions she can't answer.

This is how my life is: Boats pass through a harbor. Dad goes to work. I take AP English with Ms. Snowberg. My brother will never win his girlfriend back. Ed's in a nursing home. Later, the *Philip R. Clarke* will pass the Apostle Islands and Keweenaw Peninsula. I've checked the Boatwatcher's Hotline to see if other vessels will depart the Superior Entry. Night after night, everything goes on like this until it doesn't go on and you're in Middle River without memories. I think Keith is beginning to worry how the history I'm planning to write about tonight will turn out.

"Somewhere along the line, you've gotten smart thinking about our neighborhood," he says from the hallway.

"I want to be a writer like Mr. Slinker," I tell Keith. "I saw the *Philip R. Clarke* bound for East Chicago. The Boatwatcher's Hotline says Ed's boat leaves in a few hours."

"I've checked on it, too."

We can see the island from my window.

"Are you feeling better?" I ask my brother.

"I don't feel good about much," he says.

My parents know his sadness will eventually pass. They'll watch him, keep his mind off of things. Sometimes I've seen him with tears in his eyes.

"Turn off the light," he says. "We can talk in the dark and pretend life will be okay for Ed and me and everybody. If we look out the window, we'll see the boat. On the pilothouse and smokestack, we'll just be able to make out the white range lights, the red and green lights to port and starboard. This time, it'll be the *Stimson*."

"It's 10:30. The *Stimson* doesn't leave till midnight."

"You're right," Keith says. "I can hold on."

"What's 'the pattern bright moonlight makes on a large body of water'?" I ask.

"Moonglade. . . . We'll always remember Ed, won't we?" Keith asks. "Will you and me always be remembered?"

"Does Al forget his brother? Al can't. Nor can we let each other go."

"That's reassuring," my lost brother says, but I don't know whether he means it. "Do you think someday I'll forget that we sat here with the lights off and maybe it snowed toward morning?"

"You won't forget. I'll write it down. We're like a branch on a tree that took seed here long ago. Who was the first person in our family to hike over to the island and the old lighthouse in wintertime?"

"I don't know. You're the surveyor. Keep thinking about all of this. I'll check your observations before you turn in your assignment. Do you want a map of tonight's sky to see where the constellations were, Andrzej? That way you'll remember everything exactly," my brother says, serious about what I'm describing.

These lives I'll write about for Mr. Slinker and Ms. Snowberg include the people who'd placed the survey marker in the old lighthouse and those who worked on the docks and the sailors and city workers and our parents, grandparents, uncles, and all those who've lived in and visited the neighborhood.

It is around midnight when I see the snow begin and we spot the *Henry L. Stimson* heading through the bay past the embers of a fire.

"Look down there!" I say to my brother, pointing toward the *Stimson* through the north-facing window. But Keith's also saying,

"Look!" and signaling me to come to the east-facing window where Mr. Slinker is preparing to go somewhere. Then we see him in the yard heading the way I just came. "He's left the light on in his room," Keith says, which makes me wonder if he's going to the island. If he is, the light will guide him back from wherever else he goes in his mind, to the old country, to the war, to the long journey he once took over the sea to America. A light in a room in a house in Wisconsin.

A ghost writer is "a person who writes for and in the name of another." I've heard his translator describe Mr. Slinker as a ghost writer in the East End of Superior. He stays to himself. He's like a mystery from the past. You cannot understand a ghost. People think war has done this to him.

In a way, it would make Mr. Slinker a ghost writer if he went to the island and stood among the trees within sight of the fire. What if a boat passed? What if he added driftwood to the fire the way I'd done? What if he looked at my window from the island the way I'd looked at his window? For a second, I wonder if Mr. Slinker, Bronisław Slinker, the retired worker at the lime plant, the Polish author, is writing a story, a novel, an epic novel about ghost ships and inlets and how we live so close to the long, blue edge of Lake Superior.

TWO BLUE ROSES IN A TEARDROP VASE

To Andrzej and Keith, if you must know, and apparently you do since you've written me, it happened this way. The coal dust covered your poor, dear uncle. His shirt and pants were black. When he scrubbed himself over the laundry tub after work, bruises and cuts appeared on his face. I give these details because, once two people live together, you notice things. Lounging in his sweatpants after work at the coal dock, he'd say, "Bring me a bologna sandwich." On weekends, he didn't shave and wore sweaters whose sleeves unraveled. It was a mess when I married him.

This is an introduction to what I'm going to tell you about listening and learning. Though according to your cousin, my son, I'm a "candidate for the amplification a hearing aid would provide," I don't want to hear better than I do. I've heard enough in life. The memory of certain sounds still haunts me, so that I intend to buy the Bose Quiet Comfort 25 headphone when I have the money. A headphone might be a way to push away the things I can't forget.

It's early 1989 I'm writing about. Yes, way back then. The confused noises Al Bronkowski, your other uncle, and I heard when we fell in love upset me from the start. Al worked at the oil refinery, where vent stacks, smokestacks, and towers rose. Once you entered the place, you couldn't walk ten feet without flame, steam, or some dripping thing trying to scald you or turn you black. Pipes twisted everywhere. Twenty-four hours a day, torches burned off-gasses from eerie flare stacks above the refinery complex. Our neighborhood smelled like hydrogen sulfide. This is the perfect place for a sinner to work. Yet for the entire time I lived with Ed and Al's folks, your grandparents, I never saw Al come home grimy like my husband, even though the refinery made number six fuel oil and other dirty, viscous products.

Stopping at some woman's house after work, Al and she (Margot? Margaret? something like that) would do their oily thing then she'd clean him up and send him on. You're old enough to hear about sex. Maybe you study it in high school. Depending on the season, he did the yardwork for his parents that my husband complained he was too tired to do. Though middle-aged and still living at home, Al was a go-getter, whereas your uncle Ed, my husband, was tired of everything. Being a newlywed wore on him more than working on the coal dock. "Why don't you hold the baby?" I'd ask. He didn't listen, though I obeyed him when *he* wanted things done. One day I expected he'd bring home his ear protection headset from work to block out my voice.

With the baby needing his father, Ed preferred listening to his own dad complain that the paper omitted yesterday's temperature in Warsaw again. Frank Bronkowski had to face up to a night shift at the flour mill without knowing whether it was rainy, windy, or cold in the old country he'd come from. Here in America he owned a gray-shingled house, whose ceilings creaked. When I heard these sounds above the kitchen, I knew Ed was practicing his footwork.

"I don't like what you're doing," I'd say when I found him panting before the dresser mirror. "I have to look at your face if you go back in the ring."

"It's *my* face," he'd answer, throwing punches at the pillows on the bed. With red hearts crocheted on the front, they were a wedding gift from his manager.

To top off this cozy scene, in the room a stovepipe had once intruded through the blue-green walls. Covered with plaster and painted over, the circular outline reminded me of how cold the room must've been in 1890 or so with just a coal stove to heat the second floor. I stayed up there to smooth the pillows, the baby on my lap. Downstairs, Evelyn yakked, Al played a record about Marine Corps boot camp (which he'd gone through years before), and Frank read his Polish newspapers aloud. Always a din in the house.

After getting married, I couldn't tolerate such noise. Your grandma's opening the oven door or Al's running the bathroom faucet set me on edge. The way to get through this is to recall my life from back then, to unrepress repression. Keith and Andrzej, something dreamlike—something aural, otic—happened to me when I lived there. Your long-lost Aunt Adele, I was once a gentle woman. But something affected my hearing.

This house. What a mysterious place to a young married woman! You're single one moment, the next, you're wandering someone else's rooms. A white-framed picture window looked out on East Fourth Street. Smaller panes stood inside of this window. The metalwork on the front door swirled about a gothic "B." Given the dusty ore docks, flour mill, and putrid-smelling refinery in Superior, you can see why the people in our neighborhood and other neighborhoods coughed and wheezed. The "B" could've stood for "Bronchitis." Above the front door was an address in tin numbers. The house's asphalt siding matched the color of the garage's gray shiplap siding. You'd expect an immigrant to buy a place like this as soon as he could; and when I describe it, I'm not criticizing Frank Bronkowski. He's your grandfather, after all, a kind, decent, hard-working man. But couldn't he have understood what was happening in his house?

I remember every sound. As I examined the place where the stovepipe entrance had been plastered over, I also remember the house pulling away from itself. I was sure it would collapse in reverse of how it was built, rafters, joists, studding, and laths tugging free, nails pulling out, each making a regretful sound the way I regretted what I was doing to my in-laws. Blame me for their sorrow, for the gray that came into their hair, which occurred when I wanted to escape hearing. This is what I'd think: *You must save me, dear Frank. Unless Evelyn and I*

*drive to the A&W for root beer floats, I go nowhere. I make beds, dust
rooms, wash dishes, and care for my one-year-old boy. You know I've gotten a bum deal marrying your son. After the nuptials, I make him work
at the coal dock as punishment for my pregnancy. He isn't ashamed of
working there. He can wash off the coal dust.*

"When can we get our own house?" I'd ask your Uncle Ed.

"I'm going out," he'd say.

"Where? Four nights a week you leave me. No boxing," I'd say.
The dusty wrinkles on his face made it look as though he couldn't rid
himself of coal-black thoughts about me.

You probably think the world of your two uncles, but *you* wrote
me, asking ME to dredge up the past. You're old enough to hear it.
Al the lover, Al the veteran, the ex-Marine was a dry August field in
flame. I was the grass piled high in the middle of the field. His work
shirts smelled like refinery effluents and smoke. But, oh, he was a
handsome one destined for more than the refinery. He had such
black hair and dark eyes. His work clothes, his going-out clothes,
everything he put on looked as though tailored for him, the refinery
man. He was smooth. He was going places at work. I've written too
much about the refinery, though, the steam, the dripping. Still, today
when I drive by an asphalt plant here in Cudahy, a Milwaukee suburb,
I think of Al.

How many good smells permeated my life back then, too: The
wildflowers beside the railroad tracks. The baby's powder and shampoo. The bottle of perfume Al bought me and that nobody but the
neighbors took seriously as meaning anything was going on between
us. Al gave me two blue roses in a teardrop vase. Life was a whirlwind,
I tell you.

It was four one morning, everyone asleep, when he came to me.
Alphonse had heard something. A man gives me blue roses in a teardrop vase and pretends he's surprised when I'm waiting for him. Over
the basement windows, the blue plastic curtains cast a strange light
on the washing machine. In one corner, the coal bin that you must
recall from visiting the house yourselves had been whitewashed. Coal
was no longer stored in it now that the furnace burned natural gas.

Leftover linoleum covered the floor. The room was 6 × 8 feet. Your grandma stored canned goods down there.

"Move in here!" I said as the house pulled away at itself. I feared the walls would collapse if Ed found me with Al.

From where we stood beneath the naked lightbulb, our silhouette fell on the coal bin walls. Al and Adele, two blue roses. You two nephews might just as well know this.

A week later, I said, "We can't go on."

He held me like he had before. We kissed. He took my hands. He whispered of the lack of true love. "Oh, Al, how you've suffered," I said.

One night when he came to me, I asked, "Can you hear it?"

I brushed the bulb in the coal bin with my hand. It swung from light to dark.

"Are you hearing something I'm not?"

"You aren't hearing what I do, Al? I don't believe you. I hear the noises at night."

In daylight, however, everything changed in the house. No cracks made feathered paths along the upstairs walls then. No peeling labels curled on the canned goods your grandmother stored in the basement.

It's crazy, all right. Your aunt Adele, I still might be a little crazy. Along with the Mexicans and Central Americans, I attend mass at the Basilica of St. Josaphat downtown when I come in from the suburbs. I go to watch the Polish immigrants who still attend mass there bow and pray in a sibilant language. Some of them have buried the past. They weep that they're free of war and sorrow. Others don't weep or haven't for a long time. In Superior, Al Bronkowski with his Vietnam War or Frank Bronkowski with his World War Two were like this, as were the gossiping sisters Ewa and Hedwig Pogozalski, who were old maids always asking about the neighborhood's business. They were jealous of a teardrop vase.

I remember the details and sounds because the past is on tape. I have the tape recorder. I'd seen Frank use it to record old music, but

I didn't know where he kept the tape recorder until I found it on the shelf in the hallway closet. With everyone out one night, I placed the tape recorder on the basement work bench. It was a Sony TCM 818 model "with 3-digit tape counter." Two nights later, I put the tape recorder in the coal bin, another night on the washing machine. I pressed record to keep an historical record of sounds I heard.

At 2:30 or 3 a.m., I'd play back the tape. At first nothing, just dead winter air in the coal bin. Repressed thoughts. But I knew something was cracking and rending the house of memory.

I recorded again the next night. This time, I heard something, some *thing. Push record. Go upstairs.* When Al, who'd been humoring me, listened to what I'd taped, when he actually heard it come from the speaker of the tape recorder, he'd have to admit I was right about the noises I'd heard. So far, he'd heard none of them.

I shut myself in the coal bin. *Rewind. Record.* Then one day my good father-in-law Frank's voice startled me. One early morning on the tape recorder, he'd whispered to me in Polish, a language of "s's" and "z's." That first time, he must've spoken when he found the tape recorder running, waiting to record sounds no one else heard but me. "Tell Al to leave you—" your grandfather had said. The tape ran on, recording nothing but ambient sound after that, perhaps a creak in a wall, a spider weaving a web, the sound of memory.

I pressed rewind. I left him a message, left Frank, my father-in-law and your grandfather, Keith and Andrzej, a message. "He brought me two blue roses," I said about Al. When I played it back, I heard Al's and my sighs. "Let's record our love," Al was saying, tempting me. You could hear the rustle of clothes, the breathless words, the hurried shuffling after we'd made love, the shuffling of adulterers into their clothes.

When he came from work, Frank pressed play, record, rewind. From reel-to-reel, the tape whirred with urgent messages. "Why do you do t'is? What make you do t'is?" We could not talk face-to-face about anything. We had to repress what was happening. Maybe this is the Polish or the Catholic way, never saying things directly, edging around them to keep them secret and not secret.

"Can you come down here when I'm in the basement?" I asked him in a return message. When I wasn't there, Frank rewound the tape. With a message relayed, understood, repressed, he pushed record. The reel spun to the place where he'd brought the microphone close and whispered into it. No doubt his hands shook when he did this.

Of course, I know what it was he'd heard. For weeks, my lover and I had pressed against the walls of the coal bin as the chimney gave way. Bricks rolled down the roof's steep pitch. Frank Bronkowski heard his house falling.

"Why you do t'is? Why you do t'is?" he, Frank, begged me to tell him. *Tympanic. Otic. Aural.*

In the clear light of day, I wondered when my father-in-law would finally admit he was transmitting to me. He must have pretended everything was okay here, yet you shouldn't take a basement lightly. It is a dark, damp place where you conceal thoughts.

When Ed came home one day saying he was looking for a job, I couldn't understand what he meant. "You can't quit the coal dock," I said to my husband. "If you do, you'll have to get work at the ore dock or the cement dock."

"I ain't working," he said.

"We can't rely on your parents," I told him. "Put on your work clothes. Get back to the coal dock. Beg them to let you back."

I went myself to intercede for him. My head swirled when the train that stopped me at the crossing was bound for the Midwest Energy Terminal where my husband no longer intended to go. No thanks. They didn't want him there, they said. Ed and I lived with his parents. We had no cash. He had a boxer's robe bought with his last check. He said he'd model it. He smoothed the pillows so that we could make love with the robe beneath us. This is when I began thinking that a Ford Galaxie with a tank full of gas could take a mother and her child a long, long way. I left the room when Ed laid his robe on the bed.

"Dad, get down here! The basement!" Ed said. After he'd looked and looked, he found me in the shadows. Frank and Evelyn, my parents-in-law, hurried down. It was an emergency. "Why you have done this?" Frank asked me. For the first time, we didn't talk via tape recorder. "Why you have done this to an old man?" He was also speaking to Alphonse, the other son, as though Al were here and not working at the refinery.

"*You* know," I said, turning on the tape recorder. "Al did it with me." Our recorded love words mixed with my father-in-law's prayers and exclamations. By now, Ed, my tough guy husband, had run upstairs—to do what, weep, pray, shadow box? In the shell of the walls, something was happening. It isn't natural to communicate via thin strands of audiotape.

"I have savings bond for you," my father-in-law said.

All the years of laboring in the mill after leaving the old country, and Frank Bronkowski couldn't escape the war and wanted to send *me* away to escape it. With a pencil stub Evelyn had left down there, he scribbled all over on the shelving paper calculations regarding money. I cried, knowing I'd hurt him and Evelyn.

This was Frank's farewell to your aunt Adele. Always remember, my nephews, that your grandfather was a good man beneath that gruff way of his. He gave me his Ford Galaxie, telling me he could walk to work and didn't need a car. He gave me the tape recorder and savings bonds. Al, my lover, followed me to Milwaukee that year. But the Milwaukee story is for another time. No, I'll tell a little of it. He came to live with me, but it didn't work.

A week later when Ed, my husband, went out to do his roadwork, I took the car. The baby settled in, our things in the back seat, I left Fourth Street. When I saw Ed, fists whipping the wind as he ran, I whispered, "*Sto lat!* May you live to be one hundred," though back then I never meant for him to live so long in the condition he's in, which I hear isn't good.

I'm resigned to the things that've happened with Al, the refinery man. Al! Always Al! Now much older, I grow uncomfortable with the workings of the inner ear. How many people won't listen when you're telling them what you've heard?

As I understand it, the outer ear captures sound. The middle ear changes it into mechanical energy. The inner ear converts the energy into nerve impulses. On a diagram of the ear, you can see the eardrum, hammer, anvil, tympanic cavity, cochlea, and other membranes and nerves. My hearing was the clearest in that house. I'm glad someone was at the other end of the tape recorder to confirm what I'd heard and said. Maybe a hundred years earlier, the house had already observed the anxiety of owners. Let's say the foundation was a grave lie told to a spouse. Let's say the rooms broke the spirit of children with big dreams. I'm not the first to have heard the grief of wood, a house brooding in sorrow.

From my union with your uncle Ed, I have a son whom I've protected from the worst. His employer has opened outlets around Wisconsin, Minnesota, and Michigan. You've seen the fliers: Beneath a picture of Frankie Bronkowski, a young adult, the ad reads, "Find out what you are hearing. We will perform screenings at no charge for the first 50 callers to determine if you are a candidate for amplification. *Free audiometric testing.*" There's my twenty-two-year-old son with a headset on. He's pretending to listen to the faint sounds which in an audiometric test are sometimes just below the range of hearing.

Despite the discounts my son promises, I want no BluLink H-Series Hearing System, "the most advanced technology" the company sells. In Cudahy, I need to be left alone.

"Put on the headset for a test. You might be a prime candidate for amplification, Mother," he says.

When I get him to quit asking me, afraid of what I'll hear if I take the test, I go back to my TV reruns, *The Donna Reed Show, Ozzie and Harriet, This Is Your Life*. I keep the volume low so as not to disturb people in other apartments. I've heard them tell secrets that they shouldn't, not that I intend to know *everything* like my long-ago neighbors, Ewa and Hedwig Pogozalski, did. Whenever they learned something about me, they'd run to tell the priest.

There's a saying that your grandfather mumbled, "Jest to cnota nad cnotami, trzymać, język za zębami . . . It's a virtue above all virtues to keep one's tongue behind one's teeth." That never happened with the two love-starved neighbors, Ewa and Hedwig. They blabbed to anyone who listened. They told about the teardrop vase. They told about the plastic curtains they'd peeked through to see me in the arms of your uncle Al. There was once this house. It had two main stories plus an attic and a basement. It had gray shingles. Why have I told you this? Because your hearing is good. You don't need an audiometric test.

I saw Ed when he was in his forties. That evening, he'd climbed into the ring for a fight in a hole-in-the-wall gym in Wauwatosa. I heard he might live to be one hundred. His body's in shape, but his mind is shot. What a mess he'd become! I didn't think a face could look like that. They shouldn't have allowed him to box. "Why you do t'is?" I should have asked like his father had once asked me. The blue silk robe with the white trim and his nickname in white on the back looked ragged. A seam hung from the old robe. It looked like it'd been on the floor of locker rooms in many broken-down places. There was blood on it.

I was standing to the side of the hall where he couldn't see me. What would it have mattered when he was so far gone by then? That was my boy's dad, the man the future hearing consultant had gone up north to visit as a child. I will confess this much to you two boys, you nephews of Edward Bronkowski: Sometimes I get nostalgic for the days when he and I believed in the future and knew we were happy and knew that those skies as blue as the big lake were meant for us.

I want you to tell him all this, Keith and Andrzej. Read him this: Oh, Eddie, why didn't we try harder when we were young and married and the stars swirled above? Why didn't we whisper our dreams to each other? We had two or three passionate nights after we first met. One was the night our son was conceived. I didn't need to get sick like I did. We could've had many sons if that was your desire. Oh, Ed, we could've bought a house and looked after your parents and let Al go his way, no matter how handsome he was. It would have been enough for us, what we had together. Then when we were old like now, we could have taken the amplification test so we'd never have been out of hearing of each other.

How did it happen that we let the tape go on too long, or not long enough? What was recorded on it that we never heard? *Love now!* Is that what it said? *Don't let days pass without loving others? Forsake Al? Cherish little Frankie?* Lightbulbs, whispered prayers, blue roses in a teardrop vase.

Stop.

Play.

Rewind.

Why didn't we let the tape go on until we heard the sounds that meant something to us alone, two young lovers? Had we listened, the answer would have come to us. The sounds I hear now do me little good. They are just amplified noises of the rending and creaking of the house of life.

You tell him what I've written here, Keith and Andrzej, tell him it all just the way I've written it to you and just the way it happened.

Stop.

Play.

Rewind.

ACKNOWLEDGMENTS

I am grateful to George Gott and Thomas Napierkowski for believing, long ago, that I had something of value to write. More recently, Nick Hayes, Jo Mackiewicz, and Jayson Iwen have inspired and encouraged me. Thank you to Barton Sutter and Mike Longrie for critiquing an early version of the manuscript and to Tom Johnson for his perceptive reading of a later version. Thanks also to Ann Cleary for our long talks about books. As always, I am most indebted to Elaine, my wife, for her love and support.

The following stories appeared in literary magazines, some in much different form. "Tributaries" was first published as "The Rural Route" in *Tikkun* (online) and later in Russian translation in *Literratura*; "The Eve of the First" was published in *The Literary Review*; "The Six Purposes of Drill" in *War, Literature & the Arts*; "Prospects" in *Rosebud*; and "Port of Milwaukee" in *Great River Review*. "The Second Cook on the *Henry L. Stimson*" and "They That Go Down to the Sea," the latter entitled "The Maritime Trade," appeared in *Great Lakes Review*; "Moonglade" in *Chronicles: A Magazine of American Culture*; and "This Is Your Life" as "I Want to Be a Nudist" in *Hawaii Review*.